OLD KYLE'S BOY

OLD KYLE'S BOY

FRANK RODERUS

DOUBLEDAY & COMPANY, INC.
GARDEN CITY, NEW YORK
1981

Library of Congress Cataloging in Publication Data

Roderus, Frank.
  Old Kyle's boy.

  I. Title.
PS3568.034604   813'.54
           ISBN: 0-385-15937-4
Library of Congress Catalog Card Number: 80-1661

First Edition

For Merle and Bea Richardson with love

CHAPTER 1

"You came back."

"I said I would."

"The talk around town was that you wouldn't be back this time."

"Wishful thinking," I told her. I tried to make it sound casual and kind of offhanded but we both knew it was not.

"Don't talk like that, Cyrus Tetlow. Just you quit it now." She smacked the counter with the heavy wooden scoop she was holding and gave me a good and proper glare. "Just quit it."

I was able to give the look back for maybe all of half a second before I started to grin. Couldn't help it, I just had to. "See what I mean? I haven't been back five minutes, and the first person I talk to gets mad at me."

"Ohhh . . . *pooh!*" She ducked her head and began shoveling cornmeal into the sack as hard and fast as she could go, making a bit of a mess of the job but so darn fussed up that it was plain she didn't care.

That was all right too. With her looking down into the barrel I could spend a moment just looking at her, which was a thing I liked to do.

She never would have known it, but Laura Delaney was about the biggest reason I kept coming back. She was a little bit of a thing, pert and sassy and pretty as a buttercup, and I guess I'd been locoed on her ever since we were both kids and her with the knobbiest and scabbiest knees in the schoolhouse. I would not know what her knees looked like more recently and did not expect to find out. Not anymore.

When I'd first fallen for her, it had been all right. But that had been before Pop and Kyle, Jr., were hanged as rustlers and all the stock we'd worked so hard to put together were split up as "restitution" among the very men who hanged them. Nowadays the people of the basin hoped I would go away for good so they could forget what had happened here. And it was for sure that my tainted blood disqualified me from ever speaking serious to or about Laura. The fact that I accepted this judgment was for her sake, though, not theirs.

She tied off the first sack with a piece of twine and started on another. She had slowed down and was going at it more carefully now.

"Are you done being mad?"

Her shoulders rose and fell in a bit of a shrug and pretty soon she looked up from her work. "Till you do it again, I reckon."

"That's something, anyway. Say, how about adding a can of cut tobacco and a box of papers to the usual."

Laura gave me a disapproving look and asked, "When did you take that up?"

"This winter."

"I suppose now you're drinking hard liquor and running with fancy women, too."

"No," I told her. And grinned. "Not yet."

She stuck her tongue out at me and clucked aloud. "I swear, Cy, the habits a body picks up 'outside.' It's a wonder you act half decent when you come back."

"It might surprise you, but you don't see hardly any horns an' forked tails on the folks outside. Matter of fact, down at the Springs they're even civilized. Carpets on the floors and big ol' chandeliers with crystal things hanging off them like solid frozen raindrops, and guess what? They've got those electric lights in some of the stores. I've heard there's some in private houses too."

"OhmaGod," she breathed, though if her father had heard her he would have jumped her for it. "Tell me about it, Cy. Please?"

So I did, and without having to gild the lily even a little bit. She hung on every word and I could tell, though she never would have said so, that she was plenty envious of the things I had seen and would like to see them herself someday. The reason she would never say it was because she never expected to do it.

Like most our age and younger, Laura had been born right here in the park and had never been outside it. Never expected to go, really.

Me, I was born outside, actually, and maybe that made a difference of some sort, both in the way I thought about the outside and in the way people regarded me after the family's disgrace. Maybe they'd have stuck with a park native better than they did me. I wouldn't know.

And actually I never remembered anything from before the park. I'd been born up in a now-dead mining camp called Twomule, and when it played out Pop had given up on mining and had come down into the park to try his hand at stock raising on a homesteaded claim. I was still in dresses and diapers at the time, I guess.

Still, the land had been taken up pretty quick once people had started coming in, and as we were latecomers we were stuck off at the end of the park, away from the best grass and the dependable water with the mountains at our backs.

We'd made it go, though. They had to say that about us. Pop and Kyle, Jr., who was already big enough to help, had dammed up a couple of coulees to hold the spring runoff and below them were able to cut a little hay each summer. They even used the so-called worthless mountainsides for grazing in the green of the year. I believe Pop was the first to do this, although everyone does it now. They didn't then.

And the mountains kept meat on our table even after the game animals disappeared from the park itself and most men took to thinking of hunting as a sport instead of a regular source of food.

Later, after they accused Pop of increasing our herd faster than our cows could do it for him, they wanted me to go outside where I belonged.

I guess there is something of a stubborn streak in me, though, and while our animals might have been gone there was nothing wrong with the title to our place. That was long since proved up and patented and I figured to keep it. I had a mother, a father, and a brother buried there, and I would stay. As much as I could.

That had been five years ago and I was only sixteen at the time. I hadn't any money or any prospects, and it was for sure that no one was going to hire me on for a winter job when there was so little winter work available and so many others to choose from in the hiring. Old Kyle's boy would have been the last to be picked.

So that was the first time I turned the heavy horses and the few remaining saddle stock out to fend for themselves over the winter and went outside in search of a job.

That first winter and the next three I went west out of the great, grassy basin that is South Park and hired on as a mucker in the Silver Lady up at Leadville, going underground twelve hours a day and cleaning up the debris—they called it ore but I sure never saw anything in that shattered gray rock that looked like metal to me—after the powder monkeys blew their carefully shaped holes and brought it all down.

Come spring, though, I would shut my ears to the foreman's cursing and draw my pay, knowing good and well that in spite of his threats he would take me back on the next time I showed up for a shift. If I do say so myself I was pretty good at the job. I never liked it, working in the dark and breathing rock dust and powder stink the whole time, but I wasn't a troublemaker like so many of the Irishmen or surly like the Scandahoovians, and the long winter months of mucking had put more beef on to my arms and shoulders than most men had. I could handle the job is what I'm saying.

Still, it was the sun and grass and the warm, live smell of livestock that I wanted and so each spring I took my winter's savings and went home, using what I had saved to live on there—it was for sure I couldn't get credit anywhere in the park—while I took care of the old place and occasionally, when someone was really shorthanded, found a short-term job in exchange for a heifer or two.

This past winter I just hadn't been able to face the thought of spending all those months underground again and so had ridden east, up through Wilkerson Pass and down the old Ute trail which long since now had been a wagon road and clean down out of the mountains for my first-ever look at the plains and at a real city.

I'd lucked into a fine, cushy job caretaking a rich eastern fellow's summer estate in Colorado Springs. The job paid twenty dollars a month, and since it included a bed and free access to the heavily stocked pantry I was able to save pretty well all of it.

I was back home now with enough money in my jeans that I could afford to outright buy some more heifers even after the cost of my summer's eating.

And there was one other little thing I intended to do. Now that I was twenty-one and of legal age—old enough that I could swear out complaints and make court appearances and all—it was in my mind to be doing something about the injustices that had been done to Pop and to Kyle, Jr.

That had been in my mind for five years now, and if I am naturally stubborn I at least have some patience to match it.

So I got my usual spring supply of staple foods and paid Laura cash for them and rode south toward home and my summer's work.

CHAPTER 2

The old house wasn't much more weather-bleached or snow-bowed than when I had last seen it. It was log-walled, built low and long and really was too big a place for one person to bother with, but it was home.

The roof looked like it had come through the winter just fine. Originally it had been sod-roofed and later Pop had added a layer of shakes over what was left of the sod. Last summer I had put another layer of sod over Pop's shakes. It looked all right now.

The door was standing a little bit ajar which meant that the chipmunks and other small, furry things could get in easily. That was all right. There were enough other ways they could get inside anyway, and the food safe was lined inside and out with flattened tin cans for protective armor.

I dropped my sacks of food near the warped and rotting front stoop—I would have to replace that this year—and turned my horse into the small corral nearest the house. A few of the topmost pole rails, the ones most likely to be chewed on by bored horses, were new since I'd left the previous fall. There wouldn't be a winter go by that someone didn't shelter in an empty house, and apparently this time someone had stayed a while. A line rider or a trapper or some such person headquartering here for a time.

I took a look inside the house. Whoever had been living here was neat about it. All the pots and dishes were clean save for one crockery coffee cup left on the table. The wood-box was full, and my old rifle and few extra pieces of clothing were where they ought to be. A box of cartridges that I thought was full when I left was open now, and a half dozen shells were gone. On the other hand, there was most of a sack of dried pinto beans in the food safe that I hadn't left there. I generally bought the red beans myself, though only out of habit as that had been the kind my mother and Pop after her had fixed.

I carried the rest of the food in and put it away and carried last year's mattress outside. I dumped the fouled and mouse-nested old stuffing from the canvas cover and poked in some fresh from what was left of the hay that had been stored in the shed back of the house. Most of that had been used too but there was enough clean of it left for my bed. I got the stove fired up and a pot of coffee on it, threw open the shutters to let some light in and the stale air out, and I was back in housekeeping.

It was too late in the day then to get any work done so I chored the one horse in the pen and waited for daylight, to go out looking to see how many live animals I still had after the winter.

Getting up that next morning, though, was both a pleasure and a chore. With my lazy-man's work over the winter I had gotten into the habit of sleeping past dawn. A few more days and I would be back into the routine again.

Finding the horses was my first concern, and I thought I knew where to look for them. I definitely needed them. The horse I had come in on was a good animal, a tough little dun horse with an eager attitude and a good turn on him, but he was plains bred and I wasn't sure I could trust him on the rocks and the steep slopes where I likely would have to do much of my cow hunting. The horses I had wintered here were mountain bred and dependable.

I saddled the dun and took him up a steep, rocky run—dry already—that led south and east from the flat headquarters ground. The run carried water long enough each spring to fill a cistern behind the house and one of the three stock ponds down on the flat. It also fed a deep pond up above.

The going wasn't too awfully steep for the first quarter mile or so, then there was a tougher chute that the little flatland horse managed without too much scrambling and then it eased for another half mile. Above that was a nearly straight drop that had to be bypassed up a game and stock trail on the side slope, a narrow eyebrow trail that the dun went up just fine. I was pretty well pleased with him.

Above that face—I could remember it with the runoff cascading out and down in as pretty a little waterfall as there could be—the slopes spread apart and softened to form a dandy hanging valley. There was usually good grass here, fed by the pond or small lake that lay in the bottom. It was here that I expected to find my horses.

I took the dun out onto the fan-shaped spread of bright, new green and pulled him down to a stop. I took a long look around and couldn't find a hint of the loose horses.

After a little while, though, I noticed that the dun horse's attention was fixed on a stand of quakies down at the far end of the valley. They hadn't hardly had time yet to develop mature leaves, but already the quaking aspen were shimmering pale green flashes under the slight breeze that was moving. The dun kept cocking his ears down that way and testing the air with flared nostrils. I edged him forward and pretty soon his head came up. He curled his lip and whinnied. An answer came back from the quakies and pretty soon I could see dark movement among the trees.

The horses filed down into the flat. They were shaggy with winter hair and were unkempt but in good flesh beneath that rough exterior. I counted them down. The leader was the old brown mare that was a good producer and also a solid roping horse. She didn't have a colt at her side this spring, and she was so barrel-bellied from past foalings that I honestly couldn't tell from the distance if she would have one.

Behind her was a scruffy bay with a jagged scar along his left jaw and behind him a near perfect match for him save for that scar. Both of them were plain as pitch, not a bit of white on either, and like enough in size and even in temperament that I'm not sure I could have told them apart if not for the scar. Well, maybe that is stretching it a bit, but both were tough, dependable, day-in and day-out using horses. They could always be counted on to go to work and they would do it anywhere that any other horse could possibly go and in places where a good many horses couldn't.

Lagging after them was the ponderous old part-Belgian

that used to be our off-wheeler in the team of heavy horses. He probably weighed a ton, and one of his feet would make four of an average cow pony's. Fortunately he and his partner were as patient and as tractable as they were big. His name was Nero.

Nero's position in the file was a little surprising, though. The other drafter, Petey, named in honor of one of my father's friends from his mining days, had always been the leader of the pair whether in harness or out.

I sat on the dun and waited and kept waiting, but Petey never came out of the aspen grove. That was all there was in there.

I never will know what happened to the old boy. Just didn't make it through the winter, I guess. All the others were too fat now for him to have starved, so it would have been a predator or a slip of one of those big feet on ice or simply old age. Lord knows he was entitled. He and Nero as a young team had hauled the family down into the park. I just wished I could have been there to make sure he didn't suffer in his going.

And losing him left something of an empty spot that had nothing to do with the loss of an old horse. I guess he and Nero and the old mare were kind of like last links to the family. The two bays I had gotten afterward, swapping the old mare's colts for them so I would have usable animals without having to raise them out. The bays were just horses. Petey and Nero and the mare had been kind of like family themselves.

I put the dun to work and moved my little band of horses down toward home, old Nero going slowly enough on the narrow trail that he could have caused me a problem with the others if they had wanted to break away, which they didn't, thank goodness. I took them down and put them into the holding pasture, wire-fenced, that included the smallest of the stock ponds. It was pretty far from the house but gave the best use of grass and water.

· That pretty well shot the morning, so I had some cooked lunch and then took the dun over to put him in the pasture and exchange him for one of the bay geldings.

After I rode both of them down.

They were both of them pretty snorty after a winter of being loose and unhandled, and it had been that long since I'd done any real work myself.

We went round and round for a little while and the truth is that I had to brush grass off my britches a couple times before we were done. But we did get done, and the bays were both ready for a season's work when we were.

I rode the scar-faced one back to the house—I'd named him, obviously enough, Scar and the other one, Slick—and I was maybe a little stiff and limped a mite, but I was grinning nonetheless. They were ready to go back to work and so was I now.

CHAPTER 3

You wouldn't think that a couple dozen bovine animals could get themselves so thoroughly lost that a rider who knew the country would have any trouble finding them. Well, they can.

It had been a good many months since I had worked them, and during that time they had been free to split into as many little groups as they wanted. We had enough grass to carry several hundred cows and calves, way more grass than I had animals to eat it, so they could wander anywhere they liked and still find feed under their noses.

And the worst of it was that I really couldn't have any way of knowing how many bovines I was looking for. I'd had nineteen cows, one bull, and six steers when I left at the start of the last winter. I'd pushed them into the rough country then where they should have some protection from wind, and there should have been some browse and winter-cured grass not covered by the snow. But again I couldn't know.

Not being there to tend them over the winter, I could only find out the hard way how many of them froze or starved or were taken by predators, how many of the cows had calved or died in the birthing, how many of the calves that were born had survived it, how many of the animals of any size were not washed away and drowned in the spring melt and the early storms.

So I put the bay geldings to work and went hunting cows.

The first few days I found the easy ones. Fourteen cows with eight calves at their sides—one of the lone cows had a full udder but no calf now—and three of the steers. Five cows, maybe a couple more calves, the bull and three steers were still missing.

On the fifth day of my searching I found what was left of a

calf. It had been dead for several weeks and I couldn't tell now what it died from, but it was easy to see that something had done a lot of eating on the carcass. I didn't know whether that something had done the killing too or just took advantage of the free lunch. I didn't dare trust it to be the latter, so I started carrying my rifle slung to the saddle in a scabbard. I didn't have enough livestock that I could afford to give any away as cat food.

All three of the missing steers turned up in a high cirque with only a solid-rock game trail leading to it. How they got there was easy enough to see, but why was a mystery only a dim bovine mind could answer. They had long since eaten all the available food and a fair amount of dead wood. There was good grass available a half mile below them yet they'd refused to leave. I shook my head a little and took them down where they belonged.

I found two of the cows lurking in a brushy draw down at the edge of the timber. They could plainly see my little herd out on the flat grass yet had refused to come out. They had one calf between them—a heifer calf, I was glad to see—and both of them had been nursing it. The little thing was a regular butterball and seemed mighty contented.

If the other three cows were gone for good, I would just have to swallow the loss. It was the bull that worried me, though. I could imagine the horselaugh I'd get if I asked one of my neighbors to borrow a bull. I just had to keep looking.

I started at the highest point my animals could possibly reach and went down from there, intending to sweep the north edge of my land, move a bit south and do it again. Eventually I should find the old hermit. I hoped.

It was a darn good thing I had a little more money this year than usual, I soon decided, for much of the wire that Pop and Junior and I had nailed to the trees along that north side was gone now and would have to be replaced. It seemed to have rotted away for the most part.

I suppose I should have been smart enough to question that, but wire was still a fairly new thing up here in the park and I'd never seen any with much age on it. I guess I just kind of assumed it would fall away and go to dust the same as old rope will. I got to paying attention the day I found a bunch of strange cattle on my grass.

They were spread all over a grassy hillside up along the north edge of my place, and it took no great amount of smarts for the first glance to show that they weren't mine or any kin to mine. These were blockier, heavier-bodied animals than mine would ever be, with a lot of red in their coats and very little white. The white they did show was mostly up around the head and face instead of being splotched any and everywhere. And there was more than a hundred of them drifted over that hillside. I rode out among them and they every one looked to be yearling steers, which was something of a mystery as I remembered seeing no cows anywhere in the park that could have been their mamas, not with that coloring and body type. Finding them on my own place made it all the more strange.

My fence line wasn't more than a quarter mile north of the hillside where I'd found them, so I bumped Scar with my spurs and took a look over there. Sure enough, the fence was down here too.

But this time I looked a little closer. This time I rode up to the line, or to where it should have been, and started looking at the trees instead of the empty gaps between them.

There were the nail scars on the trees where I'd remembered us pounding them one hot summer and a good many rusty, twisted nails left. There were also some pry marks that none of us had ever put there, and some of the nails were just plain missing.

I did some further looking then and, knowing now what to look for, began to find my wire, rusted and weaker than it used to be but still intact, in tangles and huge balls now that had been dragged away and dumped more or less out of sight.

It would be fair to say that I was pretty mad by then. Surprised too.

Mr. Needham Vernor, Ned to those old enough and close enough to call him that, had run the Arrow ranch to the north of us since before Pop located into the park, and I never would have expected such a thing from him.

He had been one of the later arrivers himself and always had seemed to kind of sympathize with us about getting even poorer land than he had. As far as I knew he hadn't even been party to the vigilance bunch that accused Pop and Kyle, Jr., of thieving from them.

He hadn't spoken up for them that night and talk around the park was that Mr. Vernor hadn't ever been hit by them because he was so close and might recognize his own animals, and he had backed away from me as fast as anyone else after it was over. Still, he hadn't taken part in it, and I'd always had a better opinion of him than I did of most in the park. I'd thought him pretty straight. Finding this now was really something of a shock.

I wasn't going to get any less mad or any more answers just by sitting still and brooding about it, though, so I reined Scar back toward the bunch of red cattle and began picking up small groups of them and moving them back over where they belonged.

I got another surprise when I did that. These cattle weren't wearing the Arrow brand.

It had looked enough like the Arrow that I hadn't really paid much attention the first time through, but the Arrow was made ⟩—→, an easy mark to make whether you had a forged iron or just a piece of hot metal. These red steers were wearing a →→→→ which I guessed would be read as a Lazy Pine Tree and which very handily covered the old Arrow mark, especially since any time you use that much hot iron you are going to get a lot of blotching and blurring under the best of circumstances. I was awfully glad to note that the Lazy Pine Tree would *not* cover the 𝕂 or KT connected that I had inherited from Pop.

What with one thing and another I was near mad enough to cuss by the time I had half of those red steers put back over the line. So I was already in a sulky mood and was slouching in my saddle going back for another gather of them, when some fellow I'd never seen before rode up out of the trees below me and started hollering.

"What the hell are you doing with those beeves?" he demanded to know.

I pulled Scar to a halt and waited for the rider to come up to talking distance before I answered. And even then I took the time to roll a smoke and stare on him some first, so he would know I didn't have to get anxious about a darn thing he might ask. He was a big, rough-looking fellow and was looking as belligerent as all get-out.

"I'm getting these things off of my grass and over to where I figure they must belong, mister. An' if they're yours I will expect you to do the rest of the work of moving them."

"The hell I will," he said. He kneed his horse up close to mine and waved a balled fist toward me as if that was supposed to be frightening.

He was big enough, I guess, but, shoot, I'd wintered underground too often to be afraid of a man's fists. Once the snow comes heavy you can be months locked into the tunnels and barracks with a bunch of other fellows who are just as bored and just as boring as yourself. After a while one starts to grate pretty hard on the other's nerves and from time to time it all blows out in a fistfight—above ground, never under—that can take off as quick as the rock-smashing powder charges. And unlike most cowhands, a miner sees nothing at all wrong with using his hands in a fight. Or his feet, teeth, elbows, or knees either. So I wasn't exactly a newcomer to the rough-and-tumble stuff.

I knew Scar well enough to be sure he wouldn't go too awful far if I left him, so I grunted my acceptance of the man's offer and sailed off my saddle smack onto him.

I was mad enough to think he was a just-fine way to get rid of some of it, and I was already clawing and mashing on him before we ever hit the ground.

CHAPTER 4

"Are you going to lose it?"

He felt of his jaw, winced and very cautiously probed inside his mouth with a stubby, none too clean finger. "I'm not sure. There's a couple of 'em loose in there. Might tighten down again if I'm lucky." He used his bandana to dab again at his split ear. It was drying closed now and had pretty well quit bleeding. "I'll start moving them cattle directly. Let me rest a bit longer first, though."

"I'll help you."

He looked surprised. "Thanks. You, uh, you're Tetlow, huh?"

I nodded. "Cy for short."

"I heard about you," he said. He probably meant he'd heard about Pop. Everybody in the park had. I guessed it wouldn't take long before a newcomer would hear too. "One of the things I heard was that you was gone for good this time," he added.

"Is that why you moved in on my winter range?"

He gave me a squint-eyed look of open curiosity. "Winter range? Ain't you got that kind of upside down like? Most people call the high country their summer range."

"It'd be mine, too, if I had enough animals to matter and all year to work them in. This way just happens to work out better for me right now. And I seem to recall that I asked you a question."

He started to give me a gap-toothed grin but backed off of it. Must have hurt him. Judging from the ivory already missing he wasn't exactly a stranger at taking a lick in the jaw. "They aren't exactly my animals," he said, "so the notion wasn't exactly mine, see. But I guess young George had something like that in mind. Yeah, I'd say he prob'ly did."

"Who?"

"Young George," he said impatiently, as if I certainly should have known such an obvious piece of information. "George Piersall Ryal, Jr. *Young* George. His daddy's known as Big George but nobody wouldn't dare to call the son an' heir Little George."

"I never heard of either of them," I told him quite truthfully.

"Damn, Tetlow. I s'pose I'll believe you since you say it, but . . . damn." He shook his head. "Big George is *some* down Pueblo way. He runs cows from there west past Canon and up the plateau near to Salida."

I'd never been down that way but even I knew that that was quite a chunk of country. "All that and he wants my little place too?" I asked.

"Not him," the man said, "but young George seems to. Last year he got some sort of bee in his bonnet about wanting to make good on his own. So Big George bought him this place up here off a fellow named Vernon or . . ."

"Vernor," I corrected.

"Yeah. Him. Anyway, the old man handed him the title to the place and some animals to stock it an' said 'have at it' or words to that effect. So here we all come. Young George is bound an' damn determined to make good with the place an' show his pa he can cut it on his own."

I grinned and looked around at those big-bodied red steers and then down the slope toward my distant little patch of decent grass and my couple dozen hard-come-by animals. "On his own, huh?"

The rider I'd just been fighting with did manage an answering smile this time. "For him it is."

I shrugged. "Come to think of it, I guess I can't say anything against him. I was left my place free and clear. He just had some beeves thrown into the deal."

"Speakin' of which, I reckon I'm ready to crawl back up into the saddle now if you are."

I held a hand out to help him up off the ground. "You never told me your name."

"Jess Baker."

He came to his feet and we shook before we broke our hands apart. "It's a pleasure, Jess Baker. I don't guess I'll mind having you for a neighbor at all."

He bobbed his head, a little too sharply for comfort judging from the expression that flickered across his face. He grinned. "Not quite yet. Listen, Cy, I'll tell young George you're back. I'm sure that soon as he knows he'll send the crew up to build back the fence we tore down. It's just that we was told you'd gone."

"No harm done," I said. I turned to gather up Scar and tossed my reins onto his neck ready to mount. "Say, Jess, you haven't seen anything of a liver-spotted old longhorn bull, have you? He's wearing a KT connected on the right hip." I swung aboard the horse and turned back in time to catch Jess with a sheepish look on his face.

He took his hat off and rubbed at his forehead, though it wasn't hot enough for a good sweat. "I, uh, I guess I'll talk to young George about that too. Okay?"

"What happened?"

Jess looked clearly embarrassed. "Well it's, you know, springtime. An' that fence down. You know how it is."

"Go on."

"Yeah, well, he came down on our side of the line, see. An' he got into our herd of stockers." Jess apparently couldn't help but grin a little at that point. "That ugly old long-legged scrounge of yours gored hell out of two of Big George's expensive Hereford bulls before we got to him."

"Oh, jeez."

Baker began to look embarrassed again. "Well yeah, we, uh, we kind of shot him." He made a sour face. "Tough-eating old bastard too. All gristle an' sinew. We threw most of him out."

Hoo boy, I thought. Just what do you say to something like that. As calmly and as patiently as I could, I said, "Jess, I've got to tell you, fella. I don't have but a handful of cows, and it's taken me five years to put those few together. If I don't have a bull, if I can't get any increase from my cows, I'm pretty well done for. I really needed that old bull, Jess."

"Look, I . . . I'll talk to young George about it. I can't promise to replace him for you, Cy. None of these is mine to give away. But I can promise you I'll explain it to him. All right?"

"I couldn't ask for fairer than that," I said. And I couldn't.

"All right then. Let's go move some steers."

Jess got onto his horse and we got to work. We worked fine together and, with two of us to squeeze them, it took no time at all to gather the rest of the steers and put them back over onto the Lazy Pine Tree where they belonged.

It was coming dark when we parted.

"I'll talk to young George the next time I see him, Cy. I'll let you know what he says."

"Thanks, Jess. Don't go falling off any hillsides on your way home now. See you."

Jess Baker lifted his hand and reined away. He quickly disappeared into the timber, and I turned Scar toward home and the cold stove waiting for me there.

I didn't mind that, though. I was well used to it for one thing. And I felt like I had made a friend this day. That was a rare thing and a pleasing one. I felt almighty good riding home that evening.

CHAPTER 5

I really expected to see Jess again that next evening, but I didn't, nor the following evening either. That day I did have some luck, though. I found another of the missing cows, alive and with a healthy bull calf at her side to boot. I drove them down with the rest and branded and cut the calf and felt the day well spent.

The next morning I decided I was foolish to waste myself in worrying about Jess Baker. He would come when he came and I couldn't do a thing to change it. I went through the things in my pantry looking for an excuse and found one in a tin of baking powder that I had let tip over and spill. Now I didn't actually use the stuff more than once or twice a month, but I decided my supply of it was just too, too short. I definitely needed to go to town for some more.

The little dun horse hadn't been used for a while, so I saddled him and took off north and west. I was there before noon. Naturally the first place I had to go was Delaney's store.

Like most such places away from the city and out where a merchant can't much specialize if he expects to make a living, Delaney's place offered something of just about everything. It wasn't a very big building, smaller than my house, but it held twice as much in the way of goods than a person would have thought could be crammed into it.

I imagine a person seeing it for the first time would have thought he'd walked into a rubbish bin instead of a store, for things were stacked in boxes or pitched on top of one another in piles so that there wasn't hardly room to walk through it. And it was all jumbled in there in no particularly logical order. The wheat flour barrels, for instance, were in a corner with a pile of steel traps behind them, and a collection of axes and hoe handles leaned up against them. The cornmeal and sugar, much more popular, were against the back wall near the counter.

The thing was, though, that ten years before or ten years in the future those same things would be in the same places. So nobody ever had any trouble finding what he wanted.

I took my red-and-white can of baking powder from its shelf near the front door and looked around at all the things I didn't need, some of which I wanted in spite of knowing that.

What I was mostly looking for wasn't there. Instead it was Mr. Delaney who was standing behind the counter. I went ahead and said hello, knowing I would get nothing more than a grunt in return and not a very welcoming grunt at that. Mr. Delaney might be willing to do business with me but he didn't have to like me too. I think if the place had had a back door I'd have been required to use it.

I gave up rubbernecking in search of Laura. If I got obvious about it, he would notice and maybe take out on her what he felt about me. I set the can on the counter and laid a nickel beside it. Mr. Delaney gave me back two cents change.

"You go on home, boy," he said, surprising me that he had bothered to speak. "No need in you hanging around here this evening."

Well here it was not yet noon and my place hours of riding away, and he was worried about me still being in town at night? That got my curiosity up where I might otherwise have just gone on. "Why should I want to stay anyhow?" I asked him.

Mr. Delaney blinked twice. For him that was the same as anyone else rolling his eyes and dropping down in a swoon. Mr. Delaney's expression was more or less permanently set in a sour frown with about the same warmth as a lizard might offer.

And no, that isn't hardly fair to the man. I can remember the summers back when I was ten, twelve, fourteen, like that, when I would be invited along with the Delaney family to drive out beside the slow, sluggish stream that was supposed to be the headwaters of the famous Platte, and we would spend long afternoons in the sunshine, splashing in the shal-

low water and whooping like wild Indians and stuffing ourselves on all the good things we discovered in the big baskets
Mrs. Delaney had packed.

That had been Laura and her older brother Jack who was a
year older than me and the youngest one, Tim, who would be
eighteen or nineteen now I guessed, and whoever else might
have been along for the day, usually boys as Laura was something of a tomboy at that stage and ran hand in glove with
her two brothers.

I could remember Mr. Delaney then, smiling and laughing
and acting as referee for our games of tag or stone-skipping
contests. I'd thought him a pretty fine fellow then and had
even thought how nice it would have been if Pop hadn't had
to work so hard and could have taken time with us like that
the way Mr. Delaney did.

But that had been a long time ago.

Mr. Delaney hadn't smiled in my presence in five years now
or possibly more, and I had a strong suspicion that he was one
of them who had come to the ranch that night.

"Why would I?" I asked him again.

He shook his head. "No reason."

I gave up on him and took my purchase out and slipped it
into my saddlebags. I was still curious, though, and knew
where I could get an answer.

Next door to the store and sharing one wall with it was a
harness and, out back, a blacksmith shop run by a sawed-off
little Welshman with an unpronounceable name who was uni-
versally known as Smitty, which was reference to his occupa-
tion. I'd heard a few attempts on his name before and none of
them had ever had anything close to Smith anywhere in the
long mouthful of the effort.

Smitty had once been in the mines too, as a toolmaker and
mechanic, but his lungs had proven too fragile for the rock
dust and eventually he was told he had only a few months to
live and was paid off. That had been at least a dozen years
ago and apparently he was still waiting to die any minute, for
as quick as he got a penny in his pocket he converted the cash
into liquid and drank it away.

If you wanted work done, you brought your own materials

and Smitty performed the labor. He said he didn't want to leave any valuable inventory behind when he went. Even his tools had long ago been sold and were on loan back to him by Pete Garrigan who ran the saloon.

Anyhow, Smitty would talk to me. It wasn't that he liked me, mind. Smitty disliked everybody on the self-stated basis that everyone else had something to look forward to and he didn't. The thing was, Smitty was absolutely equal about it. He didn't dislike me any more than he did anyone else in the park, and my family reputation hadn't changed that a whit.

Oddly enough I'd always liked Smitty. But then so did everybody in the park.

"What the hell do you want?" he demanded when I walked into the shop. He looked clean and reasonably well dried out. That would change soon enough, as with the approach of haying there would be a lot of harness work and smithing to be done, and Smitty's income would pick up.

"I wanted to ask you something."

"I'm a busy man," he grumped. "You damn kids are always pestering a man, asking fool questions, keeping a man from his work." He grumbled on profanely, his voice pitched for himself alone so that I was able to catch only a word or two. From what I did hear that seemed quite enough.

Kids, huh? I stood more than a head taller than Smitty now and could have picked him up lefthanded, but apparently I was still a kid to him. And busy? His bench was empty and his forge cold. When I'd walked in he had been dozing in his rocking chair.

"I just wanted to know what's going on in town tonight," I told him, helping myself to a seat on the rickety cane-bottom chair that was his concession to customer comfort.

Smitty snorted and snarled and looked craftily wise, all at nearly the same time. "You kids think I'm so damn dumb, say things about me behind my back. You keep wondering when you'll get to put me in the ground. But who is it you come to with your questions? Me, that's who."

I paid him a few compliments in an effort to smooth him off some, but it didn't work. He cussed some more and told me

what an ingrate and a liar I was and that he wasn't buying it.
I was just like the rest of them.

As far as I knew no one really believed that Smitty wasn't
right in his head. He was just a cantankerous old SOB, but he
liked to think that we underestimated him just like he always
accused everybody of wanting him to finally cork off. By now
he was about the only person in the whole park who believed
he ever *would* die.

When he ran down from his tirade again, he said, "If it'll
get you and your damn-fool questions out of my hair for a
while I guess I'll tell you, but that's the only reason. You listen
an' then you get out. All right?"

I assured him I would.

"All right, then. This is Saturday, isn't it?"

I shrugged. I hadn't the faintest idea what day of the
week it was.

"Well take my word for it. This is a Saturday. What does
that tell you?"

"Not a dang thing except that tomorrow's Sunday and yesterday was Friday."

He rather colorfully told me how stupid I was and that I
wouldn't make so much as a good lickspittle when I grew up.
After several minutes of that he said, "It's Saturday, boy, and
there's a dance over at the schoolhouse tonight." He paused
and for a moment looked more thoughtful than usual. "If I
was you, boy, I wouldn't go. Everybody thought you were
gone for good when you rode east last year. You angered
them enough just coming back again. If you start showing up
at the socials too, you might wind up underground before me,
kid."

Smitty eyed me up and down and spat on the floor. "But I
will say that you've growed these last few years. It'd take a
helluva big club to put you down. Or a rope. There's some
still say you should have been pine fruit that last time. Mind
you remember that, boy. There's some that still think that."
He nodded sagely.

Me, I stumbled out of there without even remembering to
thank Smitty for the information.

Me? Thought to be a thief myself as well as the son and

brother of men accused of thieving? In all this time, all these five long years, that was a possibility that never once had occurred to me, if only because I knew it to be so unthinkably false.

And some still thought it.

Well, by God, they could make their lousy complaints and show their lousy resentments to my face now. They were going to have themselves a social? Fine. I could clap and stomp as loud as any of them, and I just might end up having the best time of anyone in the crowd.

CHAPTER 6

The schoolhouse wasn't usually used at night, but someone had brought in lamps and lanterns enough to spill a strong yellow glow out through the windows.

There were light wagons and single-horse roadsters parked in a ring completely around the little building, and a long picket line had been strung for the saddle horses. I tied my dun with them there, accompanied by the music already playing inside. The sound of voices was nearly as loud as the music.

It had been some years since I'd set foot inside this building, but I knew what it would be like inside.

The teacher's desk would be pushed back into a corner and the musicians would be grouped around it. At least once during the night someone would jump up and add to the scars on the desk top by dancing a schottische on it.

The other back corner would hold the big slateboard on its heavy stand. One of the girls or maybe a committee of them would have spent the day drawing pretty wreaths and flowers and curliques with chalk, nearly whitening the entire, fresh-washed black surface. The back surface of the board would be clean now too, but before the dance was over some small boys would manage to slip back there and experiment with dirty words. Which probably wouldn't shock their teacher, whoever she was this year, nearly as much as they hoped and believed. The women around there pretty much all have been around men engaged in working cattle and so have learned to pretend they don't hear words not intended for their ears. The same principle applies to what they see.

The pupils' writing tables would have been lugged outside around back to hold refreshments, and the chairs would be lined along the walls, filled now with the ladies and older girls and some of the little girls who wished they were older.

The men, at least the older and more settled ones, would be in a clump in the front corner away from the door. Most of them would stay there throughout the evening like a grove of so many well-rooted trees.

The younger men and older boys would be the ones who flowed from the dance floor to and from the knot of people I could see gathered outside the front door. They were the sons of the ranchers who stood inside and the itinerant hands who came into the park in search of summer work. These transient ones came to the socials looking for some casual fun and, some of them, for a reason to settle down and stay. Mostly it was only the ones who weren't wanting much that found what they were looking for. Outsiders were all right to dance with but nothing more serious than that. Park girls married park boys and that was all there was to it.

I tied my dun to the picket rope and decided as a caution to leave his cinches tight just in case I wanted to go somewhere. I lifted my hat and resettled it a little looser and idly daydreamed for a moment, wishing I had a fine suit and a pocketful of money to wow them with when I walked in that door.

Well, maybe I didn't have such, but at least I knew I could look any of them in the eye. I took a deep breath and walked forward.

The bunch of young bucks at the steps saw me coming, but more than half of them were outsiders who wouldn't know me from a passing tomcat. The others, the natives, got quiet and took to staring.

I didn't stop to talk but nodded to them as I passed and went up the stairs. "Evening, Tom. Eddie. Rupert. How you boys tonight? Virgil. Long time." They didn't say a word back at me.

I went inside and took my hat off. The place was like I remembered. Just the same except that someone had pasted together a paper chain that drooped under the ceiling from each corner to the lamp hook in the middle.

Cletus Saylor still seemed to be the chief fiddler back in the corner, and Ira Fein was there with his accordion. Those two could put out a power of music by themselves but they were backed tonight by Lame James Harris—his lameness was in his head, not his limbs, for he was sturdy as your average ox—on the mouth organ and Carl Swanson with another violin. Carl was mighty good with his instrument in his own way, but he was really a violinist instead of a fiddler. His music was more sweet and low than hot and tasty, and the people of the park preferred Saylor's style for their dancing. I had boarded at the Swanson place a couple school terms, though, as I always had had to do somewhere, our place being so far out, and I can remember waking up some nights to hear the quiet music reaching me from downstairs so sad and pretty that it like to made me cry alone there in the darkness.

Anyhow, the dance was just the way I remembered it being, and if it hadn't been for the flurry of turned heads and rib-poking elbows all around me, I might have felt at home seeing it all again and these same people all together in one place again. For just an instant it almost seemed like that.

Just for an instant, though. Mr. Delaney detached himself from the men's group and came scowling toward me.

"I told you to go home today, boy," he said.

"So I recall," I told him, "but we're not picnicking on the riverbank anymore and I'm not twelve years old now. I guess I got to make up my own mind about such things. Sir."

There was a flicker of something in his eyes—I couldn't tell what, perhaps memory—but his face didn't soften. "Go home, boy. Nobody here wants to see you get hurt."

"Nobody? Good, 'cause I don't want to hurt anyone either. I just came by to share in the fun."

Mr. Delaney grunted and turned away. He went back to the men.

I followed him and edged into the group between Mr. Delaney and Cletus's brother Monroe Saylor. Mr. Delaney's wasn't the only hard look I got then.

"Good evening, gentlemen," I said just as pleasantly as I could.

They all scowled, and Burt Thurston actually turned his back on me. I was almost positive that he had been one of the leaders in the group that hanged Pop and Kyle, Jr.

"Don't go, Mr. Thurston. You might want to hear this," I said.

He stopped moving and his shoulders stiffened making the collar of his suitcoat rise a little, but he didn't turn around toward me.

I said, "You gentlemen wouldn't have any reason to remember, but I'm of age now. I can swear out papers and everything, just like a real person. I figure now I can start asking the law to do something about, well, like about the nightriders around here. You know. The ones that decorate trees with human fruit and take other people's livestock for themselves. I know you'll want me to do that, gentlemen. You'll want your families protected too." I smiled and said, "If you'll excuse me now, I think I'll go join the fun."

I turned my back on those good citizens and walked away from them. None of them said a word while I was within hearing, but as soon as I was on the other side of the room I could see them in conversation again. It looked like a rather heated discussion and I wished I was able to listen in on it.

I'd already done what I came for, but since I happened to be here I figured I might as well try and have some fun too.

Laura was on the far side of the room standing with her mother near the musicians. She wasn't dancing at the moment, but I didn't want to embarrass her or get her in trouble with her father. Much as I would have preferred otherwise, I knew the nicest thing I could do for her would be to avoid her.

She was looking my way, though, and I just couldn't ignore her. I gave her a grin and a wink that I hoped no one else saw and turned to study the lineup of seated girls along the wall nearest me.

There was only one girl there that I hadn't seen before, so I went to her and asked her to dance. She was a big-boned homely girl who couldn't hold a candle to Laura for looks, but I was only asking her to dance.

Her face lighted up and became almost pretty when she smiled. She didn't react to my name and said hers was Beth Sorensan.

We danced the remainder of that tune and two more in quick succession and I found that Beth Sorensan was a bright and pleasant partner, laughing and agreeable and thoroughly nice to be with.

When the musicians broke to get themselves a sip of something wet between sets I told her, "Miss Sorensan, I don't mean to be rude to you, but if I go fetch you a cup of punch someone will have told you about me before I get back an' you won't be able to accept it anyway. Probably the best thing I can do now is to leave before I put you into an awkward position."

The homely girl laughed and again looked almost pretty in her gaiety. "Lean down here, Mr. Tetlow, and I'll whisper you a secret."

I did so and in a low, laugh-throaty voice she said, "I already know all about you. Laura Delaney is my very best friend in the whole world, and she told me. But no one else knows that I know, so it's all right." She chuckled. It was no girlish giggle but a quiet voicing of deep humor. "Not that I'd care anyway. I'm a schoolteacher and an outsider and subject to all manner of frivolous suspicions, you see. The people here, most of them, don't seem to see that I really don't care a fig for their opinions, and I have great fun pulling their legs without them knowing it." She leaned back away and seemed to be pondering something. She nodded abruptly to herself and said, "For right now, though, I think you're right, Cyrus. You go ahead and do the gentlemanly thing and disappear now. And I'll act properly shocked when the nearest busybody tells me about your wicked past." She smiled. "I'll see you again." She held her hand politely forward for me to touch her fingertips and turned back toward her chair. She hadn't gone three steps before Ellie Thurston had her by the elbow and was putting a bug in her ear, no doubt one that was buzzing bad things about Cy Tetlow.

I retrieved my hat from the hooks near the door and went out.

The crowd at the foot of the steps was larger now than it had been, and a second glance showed me that it was arranged into a peculiar sort of order. There was a bunch of natives lined up across the walk while the passers-through seemed to be gathered behind them. Like spectators, I thought. Laura's brother, Jack, was in the middle of the natives.

"You shouldn't of come here tonight," Jack said to me.

"I needed some exercise," I told him.

"All right then. You're fixing to get some, Cy."

"Do you remember the last time we fought?"

Jack nodded. "I whipped you too."

"You won't this time."

That was a promise, and I made good on it with a fast combination that put Jack onto the ground and out of the fight.

Which didn't seem to have much effect on the other fellows there. They came at me in a rush and I was able to get some licks in, but it was like trying to fight a snowslide. Sooner or later I was going to go under and we all knew it. I just concentrated on making it as much later as possible and went to hoping that my dun horse knew his way home without my help.

CHAPTER 7

Whether the horse could have found his own way home or not I wasn't to find out. He got on the right road all right, but I fell off him part way there and woke up about dawn with a goodly collection of aches and bruises.

None of the damage seemed real serious. My ribs and the left side of my face felt like old Smitty might have been using them for a substitute anvil, and my right ear was crusty with dried blood. I remembered someone—I hadn't been sure who—biting it.

The part that hurt the most, oddly enough, was what I had done myself. That was my hands. They were puffed up and swollen, the skin split over the knuckles and both of them throbbing each time a fresh heartbeat spurted more blood through them. It hurt but I didn't really mind all that much. It meant I had gotten some good licks in against those boys.

Of course I would have to be careful about using a catch rope for a while with my hands in such shape and would not be attempting any fancy throws for a time. That sort of thing was why the old-timey cowhands would never get in a fistfight and most still felt reluctant to do it very serious. The old-timers of Pop's age or better used to wear gloves and gauntlets to protect their hands even when they weren't working. In town you can still tell a lot of the older fellows who grew up in the stock-raising business by the gauntlets tucked behind their belts. I saw some like that down in the Springs this past winter and knew them for what they were.

Anyway, I woke up hurting a little but in general not in too bad a mood. I had gotten in a bit more than my share, and it is no disgrace to be licked by so many.

The dun horse was cropping grass not fifty yards from

where I lay, so I gathered him up and stepped aboard. Found a few more sore spots too. I turned him for home.

I rode up the little-used wagon track toward the house (mostly going back to grass now except right in the twin lines where a few years of iron tires had cut the earth bare and solid) in time to see a lone rider and single bovine ahead of me. I bumped the dun into a lope and caught them.

"Mornin', Jess."

"Well hey, Cy. I didn't expect to see you coming from that direction."

"I went to town yesterday."

He grinned. "So I see. Looks like you had a good time."

"You can tell it?" I fingered the left side of my face.

Baker laughed. "You look kinda like a mule kicked you is all, an' your cheek is swole up like a squirrel storing nuts. But other than that you look just fine. How's the other fellow?"

"If they aren't hurting as much as me this morning I'll be unhappy."

Again he grinned. "I wouldn't wish unhappiness on a neighbor. If you like I'll help you sow that ear on straight again when we get to your place."

"Must be worse than I thought."

"It's flopping kinda loose at the bottom. If you've got a bit of thread, though, it won't grow back crooked."

"I do. Thanks."

"Sure."

"I see you found my missing cow. That's all but one of them accounted for now," I said.

"Call it all of them then. There was a carcass over in the same area where I found this one. Looked like they'd come down the same way your bull did. No sign of a calf with either of them."

"And the dead cow?"

Jess shook his head. "Don't know what did for her, but it wasn't none of us. She hadn't been shot."

I nodded my thanks for the information and before I could ask anything more he said, "We'll talk about that stuff later, after I have my fun playing sawbones."

"If you fetch out a saw, Mr. Baker, we're gonna tangle." He

seemed to get a kick out of that. But I noticed the rascal didn't promise *not* to cut.

We dropped the refound cow off in sight of the others and she scampered after them like she thought she was a race-horse. Jess and I went up to the house.

"You have a nice place in there," he offered when we got near it.

"It sounds like you've been in it."

"Uh huh. Spent a couple months here over the winter."

"Well, you left it neat enough. I could let you have some of your own beans back for dinner." We went inside. "What were you doing over here so long anyway?"

"Using your grass, of course. It come back pretty good with the greenup though, I thought. You hadn't been using it enough the last few years."

The fact that that happened to be true didn't make me any happier over the idea of someone using my place without a by-your-leave or a go-to-hell. Jess seemed to see where I was about to be going, for he held his hand up and said, "We'll talk about that stuff later. Now where is your thread?"

I got it for him and the smallest needle I could find in the old sewing box that had been my mother's. He wanted some whiskey to wash it in but I didn't have any, so we made do with soap and water.

"You never promised to be gentle about it, did you?" I asked when he was about half done.

"Not once," he agreed cheerfully. "Would you rather have a crooked ear?"

"It might've been easier at that, but we've gone this far. Might as well go the whole ton."

"Now you sound like a hardrock mole."

"I've done some of it."

"Yeah? Where?"

I told him.

"I tried that once myself," Jess said. "Over at Silverton. I wasn't getting but twenty a month and found back then. The wages sounded too good to pass up." He grinned. "I went underground for that first shift an' I coulda sworn that rock was squeezing in closer every time I turned my eyes away from it.

Next time the bucket went up I was in it. Twenty a month and the backside of a cow was looking good to me again, I'll tell you. The next time I go underground it'll be permanent."

I laughed. "There's a lot that feel the same way. I can get along down there but this is better. If it paid anything, it'd be better yet. Ouch!"

"Didn't hurt me a bit," he assured me. "That's the last of it anyway. If it don't turn green an' fall off, you'll be just fine."

"You sure know how to make a fellow feel better."

"It's the natural truth," Jess agreed. "I think that coffee oughta be ready."

"This is your day to play nursemaid. You can pour for both of us." He did. And it sure tasted good. "Now tell me what your boss had to say."

Baker looked embarrassed. He poured canned milk and lumpy sugar into his cup and gave a great deal of concentration to the stirring of the mixture. I figured he would say something when he was ready, so I waited him out.

Finally he seemed to have it worked out the way he wanted. "I talked to young George like I told you I would." I nodded. That much I hadn't ever doubted.

"Yeah, well, he wasn't exactly cooperative about it." Jess sighed. "Dammit, Cy, young George said the way he looks at it he was protecting his herd when he got rid of the bull, which wasn't where it was supposed to be anyhow. Said it was a clear case of trespass."

"And the fence?"

Another sigh. "He said you don't have no survey to show where your line ought to be, an' as far as young George knows that wire was on his place an' so he had a right to knock it down."

I pulled at my lip for a minute and said, "That's the way it is, huh?"

Jess nodded. He looked miserably uncomfortable. "That's it."

"A long time ago . . . old Mr. Vernor filed on his place first, you know . . . a long time ago Vernor'd had his lines run by some survey outfit from Denver. When we decided we needed a fence, him and Pop had talked it over and the two of them set where the wire should run."

"Young George knows about that," Jess said. "He says the old man made a mistake. Got too generous with his neighbors."

"We'll see," I said. I forced a bit of a smile. "Anyhow, it isn't your doing. Let's cook up some of those beans you left. And some corncake to sop up the juice."

"I'm a pretty fair cook," Jess offered.

"You're welcome to prove that." Which he did.

CHAPTER 8

Jess and I parted still friendly, and he rode up toward the high country instead of back toward the Lazy Pine Tree. I was glad he wasn't going straight back, for it looked like I had business there.

I was stiffened up and aching pretty good by then, so I sat down and had a smoke and a cup of coffee first. But that wasn't getting it done.

The dun horse hadn't been used hard but he had been under saddle all night long. He needed a chance to roll and scratch. I rode him over to the horse trap and changed my saddle to the old mare rather than use up one of the working horses just to pay a visit.

And, yes, maybe I was wasting time and sort of putting off what I had to do. Lord knows we'd had enough neighbor problems in the past, so maybe I should have been used to it, but this was something new to me and in truth I was reluctant to go see young George Ryal.

The old Vernor place was not but an hour's easy ride away, and the old mare made it without working up more of a sweat than one would expect. She was soft but not sloppy, and the exercise should be good for her. I was hoping she still had a foal or two left to her years.

The place hadn't changed much since I had last seen it. Mr. Ned had not been a pretentious sort of man but he'd always had an eye for quality. Once his place had started to pay he put his money back into the Arrow, and unlike most he put it into his home place as well as into the blood quality of his stock.

He had been a bachelor not out of shyness like so many of the old stock raisers but from an often-voiced contempt for women. As far as I knew there had been no female foot ever placed onto the dirt of his yard, much less into the house itself.

Not that anyone could ever have guessed that from looking at the place. Mr. Ned had somehow kind of reminded me of a fussy old spinster, and the home he had built for himself probably had a lot to do with that impression.

It was small but tidily built, in perfect proportion and symmetry. The logs used to form it had been laboriously squared and whitewashed. There were curtains at the windows, and he had even gathered clumps of wildflowers and replanted them in a border all around the house and on both sides of a stone walkway from the front door to the hitch rail.

The other buildings were of rougher construction but had always been kept neat and the ground free of litter.

It still was a neat and pretty place. The whitewash had been renewed not long before, and the only litter was around the woodpile, which seemed to have sagged and spread out from the neat little area Mr. Ned had insisted his hands keep.

There was no activity around the place when I rode in, so I guided the old mare toward the house that had been Mr. Ned's. I stepped off there and tied her to the rail.

A man stepped into the open doorway before I was halfway up the walk.

"We aren't hiring now," he said.

"That's all right. I'm not looking for work." I went on up to the house and stopped to look him over.

By golly, there was one thing I could say for the Lazy Pine Tree. They grew them big. Jess Baker was a big fellow, but this man was bigger than either Jess or me. And so square jawed and pretty he practically looked unreal.

I had heard the old expression, of course, about a person born with a silver spoon in his mouth. Well, now I knew what it meant.

Young George Ryal—and it just had to be him standing in front of me—had it all, and all of it showed on his face and in the way he held himself, in the aloof, almost haughty expres-

sion he wore. He had looks and breeding and money. And it
was plain that he knew it.

He stood there immaculate as a statue in his tailored trou-
sers and matching vest, unfrayed sleeve garters, and unwilted
collar. He might have been working in a bank instead of running a cow operation. He also was looking at me the way a
man might regard a lizard found in his bedroll, annoying in a
passing sort of way but not of any real interest.

Ryal was about my age or a few years older. I think it
would be fair to say that I took a strong dislike to him and
probably would have done so even if I hadn't talked to Jess
Baker that morning. Some people just strike a person that
way; he did me. I like to think it was mutual.

"We don't give handouts to bums either," he said coldly.

I finished taking my look at him and laughed out loud. If he
wanted to be annoyed by that, that was quite all right.

"What *do* you want?" he demanded.

"I'm Cyrus Tetlow. Your neighbor." I grinned. "I take it
that you're Little George Ryal?"

He looked downright angry. "I'm George Ryal, Jr. Mr. Ryal
to you."

"I doubt it, but we'll see. I came to talk to you about my
bull and about my fence. You haven't been acting very neigh-
borly."

Ryal snorted. "I told Baker what he could tell you about
that. Go talk to him about it." His tone was one of dismissal.

"I already did, Little George. Now I'm talking to you."

He flushed dark red and seemed to tighten up all over.
"Don't call me that, boy, or I'll whip you down into the
ground. Though it looks like I wouldn't be the first to get to
you. I'll damn well guarantee I can do a better job of it than
the last man did."

"If you like," I told him, "I'll wait for you to change clothes
an' we can try it. Right here in your yard looks like a good
place."

Now if there was one thing I really did not want to do after
getting beat on so bad the night before, it was to get into another scrap today. I was feeling stiff and slow and nasty
enough without that. But there was something about George

Ryal, Jr., that had me ignoring my own best judgment and swelling up at the neck like a stud horse in breeding season.

"Say the word, Georgie, and we'll have at it," I told him.

He gave me a disdainful sneer and said, "Get off my property, boy, or I'll have you arrested for trespass." He turned his back on me and walked into his house.

"You laid down the rules, Little George," I called in to him. "From now on, neighbor, any Lazy Pine Tree beef on my grass gets just what my old bull got on yours. You got that, Georgie? Tit for tat, *neighbor*. Just the way you started it."

Which I suppose was a damn fool thing to say, but my usual patience did not seem to be operating at the time. I was more than a little bit mad at him, and when I said it I meant it. If it was childish of me, well, that's too bad. I said it and I meant it.

And, no, my neighbor and I were not going to get along too good.

I retrieved my old brown mare and headed for home, still so mad I was almost wishing he had wanted to fight, despite the lousy shape I was in after the last one.

About halfway home I got hold of myself and stroked the mare's neck and sighed. I hadn't expected it to be easy to get our place going again as a working operation. It was just as well that I hadn't.

CHAPTER 9

I had made my threat and now I had to live with it, make it good or let it go, but the truth was that I really didn't *want* to go around destroying another man's livestock. What I wanted was for him to do right by me and me by him, each of us leaving the other alone. Even after him shooting my bull and cutting my wire, though, I didn't want to take in doing that sort of thing myself. That old saying about two wrongs not making a right has always struck me as being pretty sensible.

So I thought about that all the way home, and I found it easier to think clear on the subject when I wasn't looking at George Ryal, Jr., and thinking how much of a dislike I'd taken to him.

What I decided was that there was at least one more thing I could try before I went to doing it myself, and I would give it a whirl. And I had to make a trip to the county seat anyway if I wanted to do anything about Pop and Kyle, Jr.'s, murder. I could do both at once.

Early the next morning I saddled the dun, which I was coming to regard as my traveling horse, and went down onto the broad grassy basin that was the park. Bayou Salade they used to call it, although I don't know why.

The county seat was at Fairplay, way up and gone on the other side of the park and quite a ride away even on a horse. In a wagon it was a day's drive. The only times I'd ever been there before was passing through on the road to Leadville and that wasn't open all the year.

That end of the park is mining country and I'd heard that the sympathies of the people there lay underground. Stock growers seldom did much dealings there, going out to the Springs or up to Denver if they had important business.

I suppose I shouldn't resent the miners in the park. Indians and the old-time trappers used to come in for food and furs, but it was the miners who really opened it up. There used to be a bunch of towns in the north end of the basin, but they boomed and went under before I ever was born. Nothing but foundations and tumbledown fireplaces now.

West of Fairplay, though, there was enough mineral to attract some hardrock companies, and they did make a go of it. Well enough that they didn't seem to feel they had to care about the likes of us cow chasers.

In our turn we resented them some. I don't honestly think that is a matter of envy. Not by itself. I mean, mine owners *are* richer than ranchers. But mining is such a God-awful ugly business. It ruins water and ignores grass and eats up timber, and if a stock grower doesn't care about his grass and water then he is in the wrong business.

That, I guess, is the biggest reason why I never even considered looking for underground work anywhere in the park. Somehow it would have felt like I was going over to the enemy if I had. Yet outside, going underground was just another job.

Does that make sense? Maybe not, but it's the way I felt.

Anyway, like it or no, Fairplay was the county seat and where I had to go.

It was well past the dinner hour when I got to town and tied the dun in front of one of the two hotels.

I would have enjoyed a short beer to cut the road dust from my throat—another so-called vice I'd learned to enjoy this past winter—but I didn't want to waste money on myself and sure didn't want to spray any county officials with beery breath this afternoon. So I settled for a drink of water that I shared with the dun.

The sheriff had an office not far from the little stone courthouse building. I'd seen it before when passing through and had no trouble finding it now.

The door was open so I went in without knocking. There was a man seated at a desk inside. I recognized him easy enough.

He had always been heavy. Now he was fat. He had aged

an awful lot too since I had last seen him, which would have
been about four years now.

For as long as I could remember he had been chief deputy
—as far as I knew the only deputy too—and had handled our
end of the park on those too-few occasions when someone had
come down on the grass for some formal lawing. He hadn't
been anywhere around when Pop and Kyle, Jr., were lynched
nor at any time soon thereafter.

"Mr. Gordon?" I asked.

He turned from the desk and seemed to see me for the first
time. He pulled off his wirebound reading glasses—those I
hadn't seen before either and must have been new in recent
years—and gave me a closer look.

"I've seen you before," he said.

"Yessir, from time to time you have, ever since I was no
bigger than one of your boots."

He looked again and pinched the bridge of his nose as if
that would improve his memory. Finally he shook his head.
"You'll have to tell me."

"It's Cy, Mr. Gordon. Cy Tetlow."

A smile of recognition and welcome began to spread across
his face. "Of course. Little Cy. You're old Kyle's . . ." The
rest of the memory must have come to him then for the smile
faded and his voice died away. He cleared his throat wetly
and in a lower voice went on, "I remember giving you rock
candy when you weren't any higher than my belt, boy. Now
you're half a head taller than me and got shoulders bigger
than my belly. You've grown, boy. You look good."

"Thank you, sir. So do you."

He smiled a little at that, but not bitterly, and said, "You're
still polite too. A liar maybe, but polite. What I look, boy, is
my age. Which is fair enough. The only way to avoid getting
old is to die young. You wouldn't be thinking about that at
your age, but it's a fact."

"Yes, sir."

"Are you needing some business with the law, Cyrus?"

"I was thinking you might be able to help."

Again he gave me that small, faraway smile. He shook his
head. "Not me, boy. Not anymore. I haven't ridden a horse in
three years nor been chief deputy in two. I'm just clerking

now. Kind of like a soft, green pasture for a used-up old horse."

"Oh." I didn't exactly know how to answer that. "Is Sheriff Wade in?"

"Johnny Wade died last fall. I couldn't hardly believe it. After all he'd been through without ever once having to fire a shot at another human person nor ever been shot at by one, him and some other fellows went up into the high timber after elk. Johnny's gun went off accidental and blew his own ankle apart. They carried him down but it took a while to do it. The flesh mortified before they could get a doctor to cut it off, and I guess the poison reached his heart. They took off most of the leg but it was too late. He lingered about a week and then slipped away in his sleep. Wasn't but fifty-seven, maybe fifty-eight years old. I sure didn't figure to outlive him, I can tell you. I surely didn't."

That was certainly news and bound to have an effect on my own future, although how or what I could not yet know. As a sheriff, Wade had been kind of like the devil you knew as opposed to a new one you might not. I'm not in any way trying to say that Sheriff Wade hadn't been an honest man. I believe he really was. It was just that he never got very excited by, or interested in, anything happening down in the end of the park where the value of the soil was in what it grew rather than what it assayed.

And of course I couldn't say anything to Amos Gordon about any of that. The two had been friends for a lot of years. Also, I didn't know that the new sheriff would be any better. He could be worse.

I started to ask, "Who is . . . ?"

"Siebert," Gordon said. "Loren Siebert. You know him?"

I shook my head. "I don't think I ever met him."

"I'm not surprised. He hasn't been around all that long. I don't think he came in until some time after your . . . family's troubles."

He was trying to be diplomatic, I suppose. "Is he in?"

"No, I'm afraid not. Likely won't be for a day or so. He and Norman McAlister are making a tour of some mineral locations."

"I see." I did, too. McAlister I remembered. The name anyway. He was supervisor for a combine of mining interests. It sounded like Sheriff Siebert was as tied to the hardrock companies as Wade had been. I sighed. "I can come back another time maybe." It sounded kind of lame, even to me.

"Just a minute." Amos Gordon took a much-used pipe off his desk and took his time filling it from a humidor. He fussed with it for a while, and when it was properly fired he sat in a wreath of blue smoke and said, "Don't be in such a hurry. We got a boy to handle deputy chores down your way. He might could help you. Depending."

"Depending?" It seemed an obvious question after the way he'd put that.

Mr. Gordon sucked on his pipe some more. I got the impression he was thinking about what he ought to say. Or ought not to.

"Depending on if it's something properly in our jurisdiction," he said finally. "Depending on just what the problem is."

"And who decides that?"

He shrugged. "The deputy mostly."

"Then I guess I'd better see him."

Mr. Gordon nodded. "You can probably find him to home on your way back down country."

I raised my eyebrows.

"He works out of home to be closer to the job. You know him. Jack Delaney."

I fingered my sore ear and grinned at Mr. Gordon but inwardly I guess I was doing some groaning. Yeah, I knew him all right. Deputy Delaney, indeed.

"Thank you, Mr. Gordon."

"You talk to Jack about it, Cyrus. I'll be looking for his report on whatever you two talk about." He took his pipe from his teeth and peered into the bowl. "That might be kind of interesting."

Mr. Gordon smiled and levered his bulk out of the chair before he extended a hand to me. "You come back and see me again some time, Cyrus. Any time. An' I wish you luck down there, boy. You remember that. I wish you luck."

He meant it, too. I could hear that plain as anything in his voice. I thanked him again and shook his hand before I left.

CHAPTER 10

It was way past dark before I got to the Delaney house, certainly too late for a social call. Of course this was no social visit, and I didn't want to go all the way home and have to turn right around in the morning and ride back.

The store was closed up and dark and would have been so for hours. Which meant that Laura, and probably Jack, would be at the house. In order to see Jack I would have to run the risk of seeing his sister too. I really would have preferred not to.

It wasn't that I didn't like her, of course. Far from it. My memories of her had vexed me through many and many a sleepless night in the past. But some things simply can't be, and I would be doing her a great disservice if the people of the park ever got to thinking that I was sweet on her. That I could not do to her. Some things are easier to bear from a distance.

Still, I seemed to have little choice now if I wanted to speak to her brother. And I did.

I might well have ridden on home and given up on the law as it would surely be enforced by Deputy Jack Delaney except for one thing. That was the comment Amos Gordon had made when I was preparing to leave his office. Jack would have to file a report on my complaint, and Mr. Gordon would be looking for it to cross his desk.

Laura's brother or no, if Jack wanted to get himself in trouble by not doing his duty, then I would not stand in his way about it. I would file my complaint and some time in the next few days I would write a letter to Mr. Gordon letting him know that I had. Whether that caused a problem for Jack would be up to him. If he played it square, I couldn't create a lick of trouble for him. If he didn't, I might learn a thing or two about Sheriff Loren Siebert and the way he did *his* job.

Anyway, there was a light showing in the Delaney parlor and another around back in the big kitchen where I had eaten at least a bushel of fresh-baked pie slices and oven-warm cookies in the years gone by. I tied my horse near the pump and drew a bucket of water for him before I went to the door.

"Cyrus? It is you," Mrs. Delaney said when she answered my knock. "I thought I heard someone outside a minute ago. Come in and sit, boy." She swung the door open and motioned me toward the big table that dominated the room. It was a gesture she had made to me countless times before, when I was a kid running with hers, and as far as I could tell her tone of voice was unchanged too. The sameness brought something of a lump into my throat for it was unexpected. "Sit down over there, Cy. I have a plate of cookies here." She brought them out of a cupboard and set them before me. "And would you like coffee? Or do you still prefer milk?"

I sat and took my hat off and had to grope for a minute before I could get any words out. "Coffee, ma'am. And . . . thank you."

"Of course. Help yourself to those cookies, Cy. I'll tell the children you're here."

I started to protest, but she had already disappeared toward the front of the house.

So I sat there, feeling a little bit shy and awkward and hoping my boots were clean, and I took one of the delicious sugar cookies from the plate. It came to me with something of a shock that this was exactly the way I always used to feel here, pleased and welcome and always a little anxious that my boots should be clean enough. I guess in a lot of ways I had always imagined that my mother would have been like Mrs. Delaney if my mom had lived that long.

My excursion into such thoughts was interrupted when "the children" came into the kitchen.

Laura was the first into the room. She looked fresh and tidy and absolutely lovely even after a day at the store. Her hair was unpinned and fell halfway down her back in shiny golden cascades. She must have been brushing it out for the night, and as far as I was concerned she could have left it like that all day every day. I thought she looked even prettier with it down.

She smiled her welcome and lightly touched my shoulder in passing as she spoke a hello and went toward the big coffee pot on the stove. From the way she acted I might never have quit coming into this kitchen. It all seemed a very normal and natural situation with her.

Jack was a few paces behind her, but his expression was not one of welcome. He was scowling and quiet in a surly sort of way, and I guessed the only reason we were not already starting to have words would be that he wouldn't want to upset the women in the family. Jack took a chair directly across the table from me. He turned it around and sat astraddle of it so he could prop his arms on the chair back and stare at me in leisure.

There wasn't any sign of Tim, the youngest of them, and neither of the elder Delaneys joined us. I suspected that their reasons for staying out in the parlor would have been different ones. Mr. Delaney wouldn't want to have anything to do with me, while Laura's mother would be considerate enough to give us some privacy.

Laura gave Jack and me some coffee and poured herself a glass of pale stuff that looked like sweet cider. "We haven't seen you a long time, Cy," she said when she came to the table.

"A long time," I agreed.

"I noticed you at the dance the other night," she went on. "You didn't stay long."

"No."

"Long enough," Jack said.

"From what I heard about it, I didn't think you'd look as purple and yellow as you do," she said. "The way everybody was talking about it, I thought you'd won."

I shook my head. "Not even close. I didn't know it showed so bad."

She giggled. "Don't look in any mirrors then. You might scare yourself. Still, it was . . . what? . . . a dozen to one?" She was looking at her brother when she said that.

"How'd you hear about it, anyway?" he demanded.

Laura gave him a sweet, seemingly innocent smile and said, "I danced with some of the hay-cutters, you know. They were really impressed by it. They said Cy did real good. Sammy Conyers made a point of telling me that you were the first one whipped."

From the look in Jack's eyes I was hoping that Sammy Conyers was feeling up to having a scrap himself because I thought he was fixing to get an invitation to one.

"I'm not the one had to be poured onto his horse and sent home," Jack protested sullenly.

I didn't want the two of them going at each other on my account, so I said, "It wasn't anything to fret about anyway. I've been whipped before, likely will be again."

Instead of that letting him gloat the way I expected it to, Jack's eyes turned mean-cold and he said, "Not by me, you won't. You're the son of a thief and prob'ly one yourself, Tetlow. If I have to take you down again, I'll do it with a club. Or a gun."

His voice was brittle and sharp edged, and it was plain that he meant it.

"*Jack!*" Laura seemed much more surprised by it than I was.

"It's all right, Laura," I told her. "People can think whatever they like. They can't change any of the truth by it." I grinned at Jack and, the truth to tell, I guess I did make that grin about as insolent as I could manage. "But old friend, your feeling the way you do is going to make it hard for you to do your job 'cause I've got some lawing needs to be done."

"That's why you came here." It was Laura that said it. I couldn't understand why, but I thought she sounded a little bit angry or maybe disappointed.

I nodded. "Had to," I said. I was going to tell her that I wouldn't have laid her open to public embarrassment otherwise, that I respected her too much to do that to her, but I didn't get a chance to. She abruptly left the table, slapped her glass down into the sink rather harder than necessary and left the room. A moment later I could hear the clatter of her shoes running up the stairs.

When I looked back at Jack, he gave me a nasty little satisfied smirk. "Since this is in the line of duty, Tetlow, let's get down to business. Tell me about your complaint." He laughed. "Sir."

CHAPTER 11

"I'll check into it," the deputy said when I'd told him about my problems with George Ryal, Jr.

"You do that."

Jack smiled and said, "Sure," and from the way he said it I could tell how much effort he would put into it. About the same he might give to rescuing a sackful of kittens he'd just thrown off a bridge himself. Well, that was all right. I hadn't really expected more than that.

"There's one other thing, deputy," I told him.

"Yeah?"

"My father and my brother. They were murdered a while back. I think it's about time the law did something about that." I sat back in the chair and drank off a last swallow of his mother's coffee. I gave Jack Delaney a level stare that he didn't flinch away from—he would have been prepared for this certainly—and said, "I'm of age now, deputy. I've waited five years to be able to say that. Now I want to swear out a complaint of murder in the first degree."

"Against . . . ?" He let the rest of it hang there.

"Person or persons unknown. The way I understand it, that part is supposed to be your job."

"You've been doing some reading on the subject," he observed.

"I have. And I've asked some questions about it. There's no statute of limitations on murder. Those men can be prosecuted today just as hard as they could have been five years ago."

"What men?"

"The ones who murdered my father and brother."

"You have any names? Any suspects?"

I laughed. "A nice fella down at the Springs, a peace officer, Jack. Like you?" I shook my head. "No, I guess not. I mean a *peace* officer. He warned me about that when we were talking this over. No, Jack, you aren't going to get me hung up in any lawsuits for slander or libel or whatever."

He gave me that tight, superior smile again. "Slander."

"You've been doing some studying too."

"Some," he admitted. He leaned back and eyed me, I thought more in speculation than harshness. He certainly wasn't angered by the discussion, which made me realize how little I knew him after all these years. He always used to be as quick to explode as a blasting cap. "You know, Cyrus, this is a nice place here. Good people. Honest. Hard working. You shouldn't think you can come in here now, five years afterward, and disrupt it all. You shouldn't even try."

"You're going to stop me?"

Jack spread his hands palm upward in a gesture of innocence. "Not me, Cyrus."

"Not you then. But someone. It may surprise you, Jack. Or your friends. But I don't take much to threats. They just don't move me a whole lot."

He smiled that faint, thin-lipped smile. "No threats, Cy. No one in the park would want to threaten you. That would be childish, Cyrus. We aren't children here. We aren't lawbreakers either. Like I said. Good people. And like you pointed out a minute ago yourself, my job with the county"—he grinned—"part time though it is, is to keep the peace. Right? Well, I'm trying to do just that very thing. Just make a . . . suggestion. To help keep the peace."

"And that is . . . ?"

"There's nothing here for you, Cyrus. You don't have family here. You can't make a living here. You don't have cows enough for it, and your land won't support enough to make your living even if you could afford to buy more. Which you can't. That's why your poppa turned to stealing, most likely. He couldn't make it on what he had. Neither can you. So all you've got here is a piece of ground you can't really use."

"I've heard that sort of thing before," I told him. "I haven't heard your suggestion yet."

"It's simple, Cyrus. Your place is poor land. Too poor to make it by itself. But added to someone else's place it could have some usefulness. So it isn't worthless, it just isn't a ranch. It ought to be a piece of a ranch. So what you could do is sell it. Use what you'd get out of it to preempt a better place and stock it with enough cows to give you a real start. You'd have something really worthwhile then, Cyrus. You aren't lazy and you aren't stupid. You could make a good life for yourself that way. Something with a real future to it."

"And you think I could do all that?"

"I'm pretty sure of it, Cyrus." Jack crossed his legs and laced his hands over the upraised knee. His gaze was as smooth and calm as his words had been, and it occurred to me then that already he was closer to the man he would be in twenty years time than to the boy I had remembered. In twenty years he might well be a real power in the park. He had grown much in the last five years and for one fleeting, panicky moment I had the sensation that I had not grown at all, that I was still the frightened, confused, and very lonely teenage boy I had been the night the vigilantes took my family and hanged them by the neck.

"I think I even know someone who would buy your place, Cyrus," he went on. "I think I could go so far as to suggest I might know a buyer who would give you two-fifty an acre for your land and pay it half in cash and half in good blooded stock cows. You might even get some help in relocating. There's good grass to be had yet in Wyoming and Montana. I know some people who've been up in that country. They could give you some ideas on where to look for a place. Better grass than here, they tell me. Lower altitude. Open winters. They say it's awful nice."

"Those cows," I asked him. "They wouldn't happen to have red-haired English blood in them, would they?" The Ryal cattle were like that, but the native park cows weren't.

Jack shrugged. "Maybe some would. I think I know a man who'd sell you stockers at ten dollars a head on that basis, Cyrus."

Lord, was he ever sweetening the pot now. A heavy-bodied breeder was worth twenty-six, maybe as much as thirty, dollars. And land, better land than mine was, was worth two dollars an acre, two twenty-five tops.

All of a sudden I began to feel pretty darn good again. The people of the park—at least those of them who'd been part of that vigilance committee—wanted me gone and away. They wanted that awful bad. And that meant they were afraid of me. Jack Delaney as their south-end deputy or no, they were afraid of me. They were afraid the rope had already been woven that might fit around their own necks. I began to grin.

I stood and reached across the table to shake Jack Delaney's hand. He looked purely delighted.

"You'll do it then, Cyrus?"

Still smiling, I shook my head. "No, Jack, I won't do it. Not now nor not ever. But you've told me an awful lot this evening, Jack. You've given me hope. I needed that. I thank you for it." I got my hat from the peg and nodded to him. "If you want to keep the peace, Jack, tell your friends I'm not the one will be leaving the park. Good night, now."

Deputy Jack Delaney had not completely outgrown his ability to anger. I could see that plain enough as I left. And that pleased me too.

CHAPTER 12

I spent a couple days restringing the wire Ryal and his people had torn down. It was slow work and often painful trying to untangle the curls of used wire they had dumped, and I learned to appreciate the effectiveness of rusty barbs—and of canvas gloves. Because I probably couldn't find all they had dragged away and because I needed some for patching, I only put up two strands where there had been three. Even so it was slow work, and I could not say that I enjoyed it. And in spite of my words with young George, I spent part of my time, too, chasing red steers back across the line where they belonged. I couldn't yet bring myself to destroy another man's livestock, for I was willing to believe that those steers had never read the trespass law nor had it explained to them.

Anyway, after several days of that I was willing to quit in time to go down to the house for dinner. It had been some time since I'd paid any attention to my cows and they could stand some looking at. At least that was the excuse I gave myself.

I went on down home and turned Slick into the little corral, which would be no more boring for him than standing tied to a tree while I pulled wire. I was pretty sweaty after the morning's work, so I slipped my shirt off and borrowed some of Slick's water to sluice the worst of it off. So I was bare chested and dripping when I went inside.

"I was about to give up on you," a girl's voice said.

My head snapped around and probably my jaw dropped open too. I would have been considerably less surprised to find a black bear in my kitchen. It was for sure a girl, though, and I began to feel my cheeks and forehead heat up. I turned around in a hurry and pulled my shirt back on.

"I didn't mean to startle you. I'm sorry."

"Does it show that much?" I asked while I did a hurry-up job of buttoning and tucking.

She laughed and allowed that it did.

"I don't normally run around naked," I told her. "I didn't know you were here."

"So I gathered. I left my horse out back of your shed. Just to, uh, make sure no one got any ideas about me being here."

I finished what I needed to do and turned around to face her. "It'd be a reasonable question, really. Shouldn't you be in school today?"

She shook her head. "It's Saturday. I don't have to face the sweet little monsters again until Monday morning."

"You wouldn't mind if I sat down would you, Miss Sorensan?"

"It's Beth. And, no, I wouldn't mind." I sat. She stood. "I made coffee while I was waiting. Do you want some?"

"Sure. Thanks. The cups are . . ."

"I know. I already found them," she cut me off. She went right to them. "At least you keep a clean house," she said over her shoulder. "But that meat. Yuck. You should have thrown it out a week ago."

I shrugged. "It's just a bit ripe." Actually it *was* pretty far gone, but I hadn't had time lately to think about replacing it.

"Go ahead and eat it then." She came back to the table with two cups of rather weak-looking coffee. "You'll get sick and die out here by yourself and everyone else can celebrate the event."

"I guess they would for a fact."

"Some would, it's true. You have some people upset around here."

"I hope you don't expect me to be sorry about that." I tried the coffee and found it didn't taste as bad as I expected.

"No," she said. From somewhere right out of the blue she asked, "Why didn't you accept their offer? It sounded pretty generous to me."

"Kinda blunt aren't you? And what do you know about that anyway?"

"They used the schoolhouse for a meeting the other

night," she said. "And I think I told you that Laura is my number-one friend. Jack and her dad have been doing some talk about it too. You didn't answer my question."

"It was a generous offer," I agreed.

She wouldn't let it go at that. "Well then?"

"I said it was generous. I didn't say it was tempting."

She sat back in the chair my mother had used to use, the one nearest the stove, and steepled her fingertips. "You must really hate them."

I thought about my answer to that for a moment before I gave it, and what I came up with was a bit surprising to me when I put it into words, which I never had actually done before.

"No-o-o. I guess I don't, really. I mean, I don't *like* them. But I don't hate them either. In a way they aren't really part of it. What it is, I loved my father and my brother, and now Pop and Kyle, Jr., are forever branded as thieves, without a chance to defend themselves in a court of law. You see what I mean? It isn't so much that I want to brand those other men as murderers as that I want to take that off of Pop and Junior."

"Really?"

"Yes, I think so. Doing one wipes out the other, you see?"

She nodded. "Tell me what happened."

"Back then, you mean?"

"Yes."

"It's a long story. Surely you've heard it."

"Only from the other point of view."

"That's the only one that seems to matter."

"So tell me anyway," she said.

"If you like. Funny thing. You're the only person in the park who's ever wanted to hear it, though I tried hard enough to get people to listen back then. No one would."

"You were sixteen then," she prompted.

"Yes."

She smiled. "And you knew just about everything there was to know."

I couldn't help but respond to her smile. "I thought I did."

Memory, though, brought me down to being serious again. "I learned different."

She sat waiting patiently and after a time I started in on it, remembering that evening and all that had gone before it.

"We'd been here a long time. Since before I could remember. It was a poor place, certainly not enough to get rich on, but we got by. We worked hard. We were honest. We didn't have to bow or scrape to nobody. My mother died when I was eight. She was a good woman and losing her took a lot out of Pop. The joy was gone out of him, but he covered that over with working all the harder. I was too little to be much of a help and I guess I was something of a bother to him too. He sent me into town to school while Junior and him stayed out here. He liked to say that at least one of us was going to come out ahead. Sometimes he talked about sending me east to college, but of course there wasn't . . . wouldn't have been money for that sort of thing.

"When I got bigger and could be of some real use I spent what time I could at home, but whenever school was in session that was where I had to be. He insisted on that.

"Pop worked all the time, as if he couldn't bring himself to slow down lest something might catch up to him, and Junior was always right there at his side working just as hard and just as long. And of course I did what I could when I was home.

"Anyway, all that work finally started to pay off and we'd about gotten to the point that we were getting everything the land could give us. We were doing all right, finally. Not great, mind you, but Pop was talking more and more about me going off to school, like it was really going to happen. Then the vigilance committee came. I don't know. Maybe they just couldn't believe anyone could do as good here as Pop and Junior had done. It sure couldn't have been jealousy. We were doing better but not *that* good.

"Whatever was behind it, that day I'd stayed home working at replacing some corral posts and such as that while Pop and Junior were out with the stock. It was coming dark, and I had our supper on the stove. I thought I heard them coming in, so I walked outside to see.

"There was still some light over the Snowy Mountains but not much. Not enough to see in much detail.

"I saw Pop and Junior riding up from down toward the horse pasture. I guess they'd seen me out front for I saw them wave.

"The next thing I knew there were horsemen spilling down over that swell out there. A dozen of them or more. They rode down on Pop and Junior and milled around them. It being so near dark, once they got mixed together I couldn't tell anymore who was who nor who the men were. I don't think the men were hooded, but I couldn't say for sure. Anyway it didn't seem any cause for alarm. As far as I knew it could have been a hunting party or any darn thing. I expected them all to come up to the house for coffee.

"The next thing I knew they were all of them riding away up the hillside there. They went out of sight from the house, and that's the last I saw of Pop or Kyle, Jr., alive. And I didn't even know which of the riders was them." I sighed and unclenched my hands. I noticed for the first time that they had gotten sweaty.

"They didn't come home that night, of course, and by morning I was worried. I hiked down to the horse pasture and caught an animal so I could go looking for them.

"I found them finally. Both on the same tree. Their hands had been tied and blindfolds fixed, but their feet were free. From the spur marks on the tree they'd both died hard, without a good fall to end it quick.

"They . . . weren't pretty to see." I swallowed hard.

"I came back home and hitched the team and wagon. Buried them both out beside Mama and carved their markers.

"I don't even remember riding into town, but it was the middle of the night when I got there. I had the rifle, which somebody took away from me. I didn't know who to use it on anyhow. That was the first I'd heard *why* Pop and Junior were hanged. They told me in town that night.

"I guess I went a little bit off my head again trying to tell them it wasn't so. Nobody wanted to listen anyway. Nobody even wanted to look me in the eye. I calmed down after a while but they locked me into a shed for fear I'd hurt somebody. When I got home about a week later, all our stock had been taken except the horses and a couple cows they'd missed.

"I tried to talk to people about it but they just said I was too young to file papers or to know what was going on. They wanted me to leave and stay gone. They've been wanting that ever since."

We sat in silence for a time. Finally Beth stood and went toward the stove. "I'll fix some dinner if you like."

"Sure. Fine."

She seemed to be deep in thought. I didn't mind. So was I.

CHAPTER 13

"You don't have to do that."

"It's all right. I don't mind." She went on ahead with what she was doing, scraping and washing and cleaning up most efficiently. "Who gets your scraps?"

"Just dump them in the bucket. I'll burn them later."

"No dog? That surprises me. I thought you were the kind who'd want one."

"I would," I agreed, "but the way I've been living the last few years, it just wouldn't have been a very good idea."

Beth nodded. "Laura told me about you wintering outside." She attacked a small pot with the washrag and over her shoulder asked, "What is it with you and Laura anyway?"

"Me? Nothing. I'm not socially acceptable here, remember?"

"I thought you two used to be sweethearts," she said.

"That was a long time ago. We were just kids then."

"I see." Beth took up the old piece of sacking I used for a towel and began wiping what she'd just washed. "It was a long time before she began seeing anyone else," she said.

That was a two-sided coin for sure. I was glad she hadn't wanted anyone else to spark her. But it also meant that that time had passed. I couldn't help asking, "She seeing someone now?"

"Yes," Beth said. She stopped her dish drying and stood looking at me, obviously waiting.

"All right. Who?"

"George Ryal. He's been pestering her for a date ever since he got here."

That hurt. I mean, that really hurt. Of all the people for her to choose. Yet all I could say was, "He's a fine-looking fellow and very rich. He could do well by her."

"And you couldn't?"

I laughed and hoped it didn't come out sounding as bitter as I felt on that subject. "And I couldn't. For a fact."

Beth hung the towel on its hook and came back to the table. She sat and gave me a hard stare. "Look, Cyrus, maybe I have no business saying anything, but I'll say it anyway. You hurt Laura's feelings the other night when you came to see Jack."

"Hurt her feelings? Lord God, I wouldn't ever want to do that. I sure wouldn't ever do such a thing on purpose."

Beth nodded. "I'm glad, because if you ever did I'd fight you tooth and nail, Cy. She's my friend."

"You couldn't have a better."

"Right. But the fact is that you hurt her. She thought you had come to call on her finally. Then you sat right there at that table and told both of them you had come on business, to see Jack. It hurt her badly."

"Oh, Jeez." I sat for a time and rubbed at my eyes and did some heavy thinking.

"It wasn't until after that," Beth prodded, "that she accepted George's invitation. They're going to a lawn dinner after services tomorrow. They'll be together there for the whole park to see."

"And to approve," I said. "She couldn't ever have hoped for approval if she'd waited for me to court her. Beth, I want you to do something for me. I want you to promise me something."

She raised her eyebrows in inquiry and waited.

"You say you love Laura. Well, I'll tell you something if you'll absolutely promise me you'll never repeat it, not to her or to anyone."

"All right."

"Beth, I've loved Laura as long as I can remember and probably before that. I still do. I guess I always will. The thing is, I care for her too much to ever hurt her the way it would if I tried to court her. The people of this park . . . ah, I can't put a rap on them; they're her people and mine too . . . but as far as they know I'm from bad blood. There are some who believe I'm as bad myself as they think Pop and Junior were. If Laura took up with me, all she'd get from it would be grief. She deserves better than that."

I reached across and touched Beth's wrist. "She's already gone through all the pain she should ever have to carry. You said I hurt her the other night. Well, I hate that, but it's done. She's past it, and now she's seeing someone who can give her the kind of life she deserves.

"Let it go at that, Beth. Don't ever say a word to her about the way I feel or why I've been ignoring her these past years. Help her have the kind of future she couldn't ever hope for with me." I drew my hand away.

Beth sat for a time with her eyes down. When she looked up she said, "You could still go to her. Right now, before she sees George tomorrow. You could accept that offer for your land, take Laura and a good herd out of the park, and start over somewhere else. Someplace they never heard of Kyle Tetlow or of his sons."

I smiled and gave her a thin, sad smile. "It sounds easy, but it would all still be hanging over her head. And . . . I loved my family too, Beth. I still do. It would be awful selfish of me to leave their names fouled and just ride away from the park. I don't see as I could do that."

Beth smiled. "You know, Cyrus, I think that down through history man's pride and his sense of honor have caused him more grief and unhappiness than greed ever has. And the silliest thing about it is that we womenfolk never really have understood what all the fuss has been about. We understand honesty, of course. We approve of integrity. But manly pride and honor?" She shrugged. "Those are beyond us. We are pragmatists, practical in a way you men can't seem to understand."

"But you won't . . . ?"

She shook her head. "No, I won't tell her. I think you're wrong, though."

"You did promise."

"I did promise," she agreed. "I'll keep my word." She smiled. "Remember, I did say that women understand and appreciate honesty. I'll keep my promise to you, Cy. And because I love and value Laura so much, I'll even pray that you are right and I am wrong about what you decided."

She gave me an impish little grin that almost completely hid her homeliness. "You wouldn't want a date for the lawn dinner tomorrow, would you?"

I guess my surprise—and my lack of enthusiasm—showed on my face, for before I had to speak the words she laughed and stood up.

"I thought so. It's a pity, though. That and that I'm not much of a poacher. You're a hell of a man, Cyrus Tetlow. The woman who winds up in your bed will be a lucky one for sure."

She was out the door and gone before I could think of a single thing to say to that. Which really did not have to be all that quick an exit. I mean, if I had been surprised before I was downright shocked now.

I got my wits about me, sort of, after a moment or so and charged outside and around to the back where she had tied her pony. She had just caught it up and was about to mount. I remembered my manners in time to give her a hand up into the beat-up sidesaddle that I guessed was a rented outfit.

"Thank you," she said politely.

I nodded her welcome. "Tomorrow," I said. "I could meet you at the church. After services, I mean."

"What would you like for your dinner?"

"Anything would be all right. So long as the meat isn't green."

She laughed. "Fair enough, Cy. And don't worry. I might not be pretty, but I *am* a good cook."

I suppose, thinking back to it, that I should have said something polite and gallant in answer to that, but I never thought of it at the time. "I'll look forward to seeing you tomorrow then, Beth."

"Good-bye then, Cyrus." She held her chin high and gave the pony a lick with her quirt. She was no poor hand as a rider, that was for sure. She took out of there with as elegant a seat as ever a body might see, which is a thing darn few men would be riders enough to accomplish on one of those sideways rigs and which I certainly could not have done. I watched her down the track into the distance and wondered what I was letting myself in for at that dinner.

CHAPTER 14

My very best clothes were no great shakes, but they were my best and I wore them and rode a little dun horse that had been curried within a few strokes of drawing blood, I think, from all the repeated scraping and brushing. Not that he had seemed to mind the attention. He was stepping pretty proud and I was riding as straight-backed as a yellowleg cavalry officer when we, that horse and me, rode out from behind the buildings and into sight of the churchyard.

There was already quite a crowd gathered on the lawn there. Well, to be honest, it was not much of a lawn by city standards since there was little enough grass on the much-trampled ground and what little there was had not been tended, but here in the park it was, by darn, a lawn and that was that.

Sawhorses and planks had been set up to accommodate the foods, and there were a couple galvanized steel tubs that held lemonade with chunks of ice floating in them.

The ladies were dressed in their very best, and the men looked as well brushed as my horse had been.

All in all it was a very gay picture to behold, and a few years before or anywhere outside the park I guess I would have been as excited as a pup in a schoolroom to be going to the affair. As it was, I had some doubts. I still couldn't understand why I had gone and agreed to attend. I sure had not intended to.

I tied the dun with the others and knocked some of the road dust from my britches and rubbed the toes of my boots on the backs of my pant legs to clean them off some. I wondered if there were really as many people staring at me as I thought there were.

I stopped short of the crowd and stood there for a moment,

and the next thing I knew Beth Sorensan was at my side and I felt some better. I don't know where she came from in such a hurry, but I was glad to see her.

She gave me a smile and a welcome just like I was regular people, and if she cared at all what the people of the park were going to think about that, she certainly did not show it.

"I've been watching for you," she said. "I was beginning to think you'd changed your mind."

I shook my head.

"That's right, though, isn't it? I should have known better. You men are much too proud to back down from a thing once you've set your minds to it."

I was beginning to feel a bit looser. I gave her a grin and said, "I think you gave me your opinion about that yesterday already."

"And it never changed overnight either," she said quite positively. I was willing to believe that her opinions would not be especially easy to change over a long haul, much less overnight. I was beginning to think that maybe this was a plucky girl. Plucky to the point of plain stubbornness perhaps. Likable too.

"So what did you bring to feed me, woman?"

"Just like that? No social chit-chat first? Uh huh, just like a man indeed, Cyrus Tetlow."

"You didn't answer my question."

"The answer should be perfectly obvious, sir. La, I wouldn't dare defy tradition now, would I? I brought you fried chicken and cold biscuits with a jar of honey to sop them with and a bowl of potato salad, of course. Tradition to a T, sir."

"No, of course I wouldn't expect you to do anything that wouldn't be the accepted way of doing things. Unless you happened to feel like it."

She giggled. "Well, once in a great while, I admit." She linked her arm into mine and asked, "Are you ready to beard the lion, Cy?"

"You're sure you don't mind? I mean, you might still be able to back out without people saying too much."

"They're already saying too much. Now, are you ready?"

"I am."

"Forward then, by all means, Cy." She grinned impishly. "Forward the Light Brigade."

"I remember that one. I'm not at all sure that I approve of the reference."

She tossed her chin perkily and we marched ahead into the buzzing crowd.

It was . . . an ordeal. Not that anyone exactly said anything outright. This was, after all, a church gathering with all the kids from the south end of the park along with the families, and people were wearing their holiday manners as well as their Sunday clothes. The better element was just kind of pointedly silent toward us.

If that affected Beth, she was well able to keep from showing it. She laughed and chattered and teased at me nonstop, and the truth is that if it hadn't been for all the other people I would have been having a thoroughly delightful time. As I had gathered at the dance that night, she was not much to look at but she was a pleasure to be with. If this social had been taking place down in the flat country, I do not doubt but what I would have had a better time than I'd ever had in my life. Even here she was good company.

We talked between ourselves and nodded pleasantly whenever we saw anyone looking our way and listened to the children's choir—there were about a dozen kids in the group, ranging from small fry to kids probably ten or twelve years old—sing a selection of old favorites, and when the Reverend Mister Bartleson led everyone in a group sing, Beth's voice was as loud and as sweet as any among them. Mine, I admit, was not so fine, but I staggered along with them as best I could.

During all that time I never once caught sight of Laura or of that darn George and, yes, I guess I was looking for them. Beth didn't seem to be, but I could not swear to that. She just did not make it obvious if she was. I hoped I was not being too obvious about it either.

Come the dinner call, though, there they were. Laura looked just absolutely radiant in a soft, white dress with lace up high around her neck, and Young George Ryal looked disgustingly handsome in a dark suit that probably was worth more than every stick of clothing I owned and my saddle and bridle thrown in.

Beth, well, she wasn't any shrinking violet. She had her arm linked into mine again, and no sooner had Laura and Ryal shown up in the crowd than Beth was dragging me in their direction. She slipped into the food line right smack behind them, put on her very brightest smile, and gave them some socially correct howdies.

Laura acted genuinely pleased to see Beth. She acted not quite so genuinely unable to see me standing there with Beth hanging onto my arm. Ryal, he pretended not to see either of us.

Laura found her basket on the table, and Ryal took it to carry for her. Beth's was right close to it, maybe by accident, although I would not have bet on that. I took it and lugged it where Beth pointed, which naturally was right behind the path Laura and Ryal were taking.

"You wouldn't mind if we joined you, would you?" Beth asked bright and cheerful when the four of us had reached the tailgate of someone's wagon.

"Of course not," Laura said. She sounded a little strained, but she said it.

Ryal was not so socially polite.

"Look," he said firmly, "this has gone quite far enough. I want to have a pleasant time here this afternoon. And I do *not* want to share my dinner and Miss Delaney's company with a known cattle thief. The good people who live here may be willing to put up with you, Tetlow, but I am not. I suggest you have your meal elsewhere. As for you, Beth, I know you are a good friend of Laura's, but your peculiar sense of humor is not appreciated at the moment. Please take your joke somewhere else for the afternoon. Or call the fun ended and join us for dinner. Alone."

"I think not, Mr. Ryal," she said. She sounded perfectly undaunted. The girl did have an independent turn of mind.

"I insist," Ryal said.

"And I object," Beth told him.

"Then I suggest that, your friendship with Miss Delaney

notwithstanding, you are a boor, Miss Sorensan." Ryal turned his back and bent over Laura's food hamper.

My oh my. Now that was not a nice thing for him to have said. With my very tip-top best manners I gave Beth a short bow and said, "If you will excuse me for a moment, Beth . . . ?"

She smiled at me sweetly.

I tapped Ryal on the arm and when he turned I gave him a nice smile. He scowled and opened his mouth to say something, but I did not wait to hear what it would have been. I proceeded to beat hell out of him.

Afterward, considering both prudence and Beth's reputation, I collected my dun and got out of there. It was a shame, too. I had really been looking forward to that fried chicken and I never thought to carry any along with me.

CHAPTER 15

The cattle had water and more grass than they could begin to eat, so they didn't really need much minding. I did have that fence repair to finish, though, so I kept at it for several more days until it was done. The job wasn't as fiddle-string taut as the first time we'd put it up, but it wasn't sagging either. Without grabbers and pulleys there just isn't but so much a lone worker can do to pull wire.

While I was working a man rode by; he was too far away to be sure but from size and shape I thought it was Jess Baker. I waved and got an answer but he didn't turn up my way. I guessed that if it was Jess—and it could have been another Ryal hand—he might have been told to stay away from me. Young George hadn't seemed much inclined toward neighborliness to start with, and now that situation was not likely to improve. The faster and the farther I went from here, the better he would like it.

When the fencing was done, I spent an evening at the kitchen table with some stationery I found in my folks' bureau and wrote out a letter to Amos Gordon. I didn't want the old lawman to forget his promise about those reports. The next morning I saddled the dun horse and went to town.

I posted my letter first and, for a change, was thankful that Mr. Delaney did not hold the postal contract. This time I did not want to have to face Laura if I could avoid it. I wouldn't have known what to say to her after that fiasco at the lawn dinner.

The post office was at what locally served as a combined hotel and mineral baths at the crossroads. Travelers sometimes stopped there before they turned down toward Kester and Salida or up to Fairplay and the mining areas. A rare few also took the mineral baths but as far as I knew none of the park natives had ever tried them. I really couldn't say what the attraction was supposed to be; but whatever it was it certainly wasn't popular the way things were down at Manitou, where consumptives would come for the air and the waters.

Anyway, Giles Crocker took my letter and my three cents but said he hadn't seen Jack Delaney lately. He suggested if Jack wasn't at the store he might be at Garrigan's, which was mostly saloon with a few parts of store thrown in more or less by happenstance.

I suppose Pete Garrigan started out to be a saloon-keeper, and he pretty much stayed with that. Except for beer and spirits and the odd bottle of wine, he didn't really *sell* anything in his place. But he was by nature a trader. The man loved to make a swap, anything he had on hand against just about anything he didn't have, so you might find just about any darn thing dropped into a corner or draped on the walls or sitting on the porch across the front of his place.

I've seen bales of high-smelling furs on his floor and a crank-operated, automatic-clothes-washing machine on his porch and once—though how it came into the park or whoever took it away, I couldn't know—a bright painted, spanking-new John Deere plow propped in a corner.

If anyone walked in with just cash money in his pocket, though, the only thing he could walk out with was a drink in his belly. Pete would take money for that but for nothing else. The rest was for swapping, not for sale. Try to buy something and Pete would get mad and tell you he was a saloon-keeper and not some damned store clerk. Keep it up and he could get right nasty about it, as more than one traveler has learned. I don't think a person could buy a paper of pins from Pete for a hundred dollars cash. But swap him? That was his meat. He'd bargain a trade until he got it done even if he had to take a beating on the deal to do it. Which he did not often do.

It had been a long, long time since I'd been inside Garrigan's, since back when I used to come in once and a while with Pop and, less often, with Junior. At those times I'd been all eyes and ears but too young to admit to a thirst of my own. Pete recognized me right off when I came in, of course. I guess I was about as close as we had to an infamous figure in the park and was recognizable in the same way Jesse James must have been in the neighborhood of his mother's farm out in Missouri.

Pete nodded and said, "Cyrus," and I knew he had accepted me as being grown enough now to be served. He had never been shy about throwing out a young fellow who Pete thought wasn't yet old enough for his first liquor or about quitting pouring for a grown man who Pete thought had had enough for one trip. It was rare that a man was unsteady on his feet when he left Garrigan's, which may be one of the reasons why the women of the park, at least of our part of it, never got too wound up in the temperance movement that we were always reading about in the outside papers.

There were a few other men in the place, but they ignored me without being particularly nasty about it. I was almost grateful to them for that.

I walked up to Pete's bar and propped a boot onto the genuine brass footrail—hauled in by wagon before the railroad ever reached the north end of the park—and stood there for a moment thinking back to how many times I had seen Pop do exactly that same thing. I guess I was feeling a little bit old and more than a little bit lonely.

"I'd like a beer, Mr. Garrigan."

He nodded and drew one and I laid my nickel down.

"I was looking for Jack Delaney," I told him.

"What for?" he asked bluntly. I had heard tell, and have read, that eastern people are under the impression that western men are as closemouthed as Indians are supposed to be; but I have never personally observed any reluctance to question or to gossip, and I suppose that our people in the park would qualify as western folk to an easterner's satisfaction.

"He's deputying these days and I wanted to ask him about some deputy business," I said.

Pete grinned. "You're most healed up now. I was wondering if you wanted to put some of that back where it come from."

"No, sir." I didn't remember seeing Mr. Garrigan at the dance that night, but it certainly was no surprise that he would know all about it. I couldn't resist adding, "Anyway Jack's not the one that caused the damage. He was the first one in an' also the first one out of it. I think he whipped me for the last time a long while back."

Mr. Garrigan looked me over the way a man will inspect an ox and said, "I guess you're right at that, Cyrus. You've put some heft on your shoulders since you used to come in here. A good bit of it. And anyone big enough to whip George Ryal has to be able to handle himself. I never thought of you as a fighter, though."

"Growing up can do that to a person."

He grunted.

"Any ideas where I might find the deputy?"

"Nope. He stops in here sometimes. Wanders off around the countryside sometimes. He's only part-time with the county, anyhow. You could try the store or more likely the house."

I drained off the last of my beer and told him, "If he comes in today, tell him I'll wait over at Smitty's, would you?"

Mr. Garrigan grinned again. "Don't wanta see the sister, huh?"

I shrugged. "I'll be at Smitty's." Good grief but it must be nice to live in a place where everybody doesn't know everybody else's business, I was thinking. But I wasn't surprised and there was no point in resenting it. Before the troubles it had been no secret what my intentions were, and it was no great trick for people to see that Laura hadn't been accepting fresh suitors. Or that now she was, starting this past weekend. I was sure the people of the park would be quite pleased with the way things were turning out.

I led my dun across the street and around behind Smitty's place to the pen he had there for his shoeing customers. If it was going to be a long wait there was no point in making the horse stand tied the whole time.

Smitty was in his normal foul humor and to mollify him I let him pull the dun's shoes and trim the horse's feet. I hadn't brought any bar metal with me, so he reshaped the old shoes and reset them, complaining the whole time about the poor quality of work the last man had done. Which had been me, although I knew better than to say anything. I've never

known a smith or a farrier who had any respect for the last
fellow's work.

When Smitty finally got tired of his grumbling and decided
to put his now-hot forge to use with some work he hadn't
been bothering to do, I stretched out on the straw pile at the
back of his place and took myself a nap.

The next thing I knew Smitty was nudging my ribs with the
toe of his shoe. The place was pitch black except for a faint
glow from the dying coals in the forge.

"Wake up, kid. I'm fixing to close now."

"I'm awake." I sat up and rubbed my eyes. "It feels like
midnight."

"Not yet, but it ain't too far off."

"Jack Delaney hasn't come looking for me, huh?"

Smitty snorted and muttered a few curses, which did not really mean he disliked Jack more than anyone else. "He rode
by a while ago but he never stopped. Looked like he was on
his way out somewhere. You missed him."

I muttered a few curses of my own, thanked Smitty for his
generous hospitality—which brought on some more snorting
and cussing—and saddled the little dun. It looked like I had
wasted the day.

I took the road home, familiar enough after the years that it
would take more than a moonless night to make me lose the
way.

I was wide-awake after so much spare sleep and was enjoying the cool air and the night sounds all around me—all the
clicks and chirpings of the insects and the occasional brisk
calls and hooting of the birds.

About five miles out, the busy noises quit. Just all of a sudden stopped. And the dun began to twitch his ears and side-
step in some sort of discomfort.

I reached forward to stroke the animal's neck and I believe
I was about to say something to soothe him.

From off to my left, though, I saw a bright blossom of fire, a
wide yellow rose of flame with, at its center, a fiery spearpoint
pointed right at me. Almost at the same instant I heard the
quick, sizzling *"whap"* of a bullet cutting the air just over my
head.

It scared the horse as much as it did me. He bolted forward in a spasmed leap, and that was just fine by me. By then I was raking him with my spurs to make sure he didn't change his mind.

Behind us—not very darn far behind us—I heard another shot. Whoever it was wasn't giving up.

CHAPTER 16

Somebody hated me enough or feared me enough—or both—to want to shoot me. That was interesting. I suppose it meant that I had a really good chance of accomplishing what I wanted here, otherwise they wouldn't be so worried. And I suppose that should have pleased me. It didn't.

The thing is, I believe it would take pretty much of a fool to actually *want* to be shot at, and I don't believe I am that much of a fool. I was learning already that being a target is not a fun thing.

I was just plain scared.

No one had ever shot at me before and it was unnerving. For that matter, I had never ever heard an angry shot fired before that night. At game for the table, sure, but this was a whole different thing. Even when they had hanged Pop and Junior there had been no shooting, just those dim shapes moving in the dusk and their horses moving off toward the mountain.

I had seen fights enough before, lots of them up at the mines. But those were fistfights and once in a while really rough brawls with men going at each other with steel pry bars or drill bits or occasionally with the flashing glitter of knives.

Men could die that way and sometimes they did, but it was not really that that got to me.

The violence I had seen before and that which I had participated in had always been face to face, one man against another and the better man to win. I could accept that. Even, I think, the thought of losing.

But this was something else entirely.

This was death unseen, death hiding in the night, death

reaching out from behind my back to strike me down before I might know it was there.

I rode home that night terribly, acutely conscious of the thinness of the cloth covering my back, no more protection against a bullet than a spider web would have been, and I began to understand why the old-time warriors they taught us about in school had gone to war with armor on their bodies. Even if those thin sheets of metal would have done nothing to stop a modern .44-40 or .50-70 slug, I would have given anything to have been wearing a Spanish cuirass for the remainder of that ride.

Even after I got home I was afraid. If one of them had been lying up for me, there could be another. There might be any number more. They could be waiting outside the corral, surrounding the yard, hiding somewhere in my own house until I presented myself for the slaughter. And I was afraid.

One thing I did learn, though. I was afraid but I was not paralyzed. I could be taken but I would not come free of charge. Not ever again. Whoever had fired those shots had had his last easy ones.

My first reaction had been surprise, and I had raced away in flight without once thinking of the old carbine in its scabbard under my leg. I had put the gun there out of concern for predators, with never a thought that I might have to turn it against a human being. Well, man could become a predator too. And from now on if a man missed with his first bullet at me he could expect to have one returned.

It was not a thing I was ever taught but common sense and cold fear told me not to ride straight into my yard when I got home. I circled first and, finding no horses hidden anywhere near, still approached cautiously. I went the last several hundred yards on foot, reins trailing in one hand and rifle ready in the other.

I unsaddled quickly, my attention on the house and surroundings, and kept to the shadows and the solid protection of log walls when finally I went to my own door.

Once inside—and there had been considerable heart-thumping hesitation before I got there—I lighted no lamps but checked every cranny of the house before I was willing to believe I was alone. From now on I would be leaving locked doors and tightly latched shutters and would be sleeping behind them as well.

It was little better in the morning, for a rifle has little respect for distance and I had hunted quite enough to know that a careful man can hide himself in little more cover than a few blades of grass. Stillness is far more important to concealment than cover is, and Pop had long ago taught me to stalk close to wary deer by creeping toward them when their attention was elsewhere and freezing into instant immobility whenever they raised their heads from grazing.

Those same lessons I had once learned so I could put meat onto our table I now had to relearn from the deer's point of view, and I quickly came to appreciate how the stalk favored the hunter over the hunted once the quarry had been located.

Which had to be the key to my own survival. Once the quarry was located, I had told myself.

All right, then. If I was to be the hunted in this deadly game, it was up to me to make it difficult for the hunter. I could no longer afford for my movements to be open and predictable. So they would not be. Not again.

No more of using the public roads to go from one place straight to another. No more indications of where I would go next. Above all, no more coming home to the predictable destination of home and bed.

I began assembling food and blankets into packs I could hide here and there in the small and distant niches I knew so well on the mountain at my back. I had spent time in the open before. I could do so again and in places where no man who had not worked my land was likely to find me.

I spent the remainder of that day with the carbine in one hand and pack horse reins in the other, while I made my scattered caches in a dozen places high on the mountain. The dun horse and the gelding I called Slick I turned loose in the high meadow where I had found the horses those weeks before. When I wanted to change horses, I did not propose to return to the grassy horse trap below, for the trap, or pasture, could have been better named than I had ever realized.

And finally there remained one thing I had to do. Like it or

not—and I did not—I had to ride to town and report the shooting to Deputy Sheriff Jack Delaney.

That I really did not want to do.

Because, you see, it had occurred to me during my nearly
sleepless night that old Smitty, who really did not care
enough to lie for or against any man, had said that Jack
Delaney rode out ahead of me on the road where my
ambusher waited.

There was a very real possibility that I was about to go report the shooting to the very man whose finger had been on
the trigger.

I had no choice, though, if I intended to keep this matter
within the law. And slim though the likelihood might be, the
law was the only ally I could hope to find anywhere in the
park. If I thought at all to win—and I very much still did—it
would have to be within the law and not beyond it.

I saddled the scar-faced bay gelding, tied on enough food
to last me several days, and began a long, circuitous route
back down toward the broad, open expanse of grass that was
the park.

CHAPTER 17

"Who is it, dammit? What do you want?" It was Mr. Delaney's voice.

"I need to see the deputy."

"My God, man, it's three o'clock in the morning. Come back tomorrow."

"I won't be here tomorrow."

"Who . . . ?" He looked out. "You. Get out of here or I'll have my boy run you in for disturbing the peace."

"Mr. Delaney, I haven't even started to disturb your peace yet. But I'm willing to. I'll keep it up until I see him too."

I think even then Delaney would have shut the door on me, but Jack's head showed in the partially opened doorway behind his father's. "What the devil is going on here? Hush up or you'll wake the women. Tetlow, is that you? I should've known. And what're you carrying a rifle for?"

"Official business, Deputy."

"Oh, hell." He rubbed at his eyes for a moment and edged in front of his father. "I'll take care of it, Dad. Why don't you go on up and tell Mama it's all right."

"If you need any help . . ."

"If I do, I'll holler." Jack slipped outside and pulled the door closed behind him. He was barefoot and wearing a nightshirt that was too short for him. His legs looked pale and skinny in the moonlight. Not exactly an imposing figure seen that way. He smoothed his tousled hair back but seemed fully awake now. "Tetlow, you sure better have something important to talk about. An' keep your voice down; the folks' bedroom is right above us."

"Maybe we could talk easier in the shed."

He seemed to think about it for a moment then shrugged.

"Why not." Jack led the way around the side of the house and into the shed where they stored their buggy and harness and such. He walked gingerly across the sharp gravel of the soil while my boots crunched along beside him. In the deep shadow of the shed, he pulled himself gratefully up onto the comfortable seat of the light rig and motioned me up beside him.

"All right," he said. "What's the big rush all about and all the secrecy?"

I climbed up and settled myself with the carbine between my knees before I answered. I told him about the shooting the night before.

Jack sighed loudly when I was done. It was too dark for me to see his expression, which was a shame.

"You know, Tetlow, if it wasn't that it would cause me so much work afterward I could almost wish he'd got you." He sighed again. "So what do you want me to do about it?"

"For starters, you might find out who did it and arrest him. Maybe you haven't heard, but it's illegal to shoot people around here."

"Yeah. Right. I'll get right on it. You can tell me who it was, of course."

"You know better than that. I told you it was pitch black. The moon wasn't even up yet."

"Uh huh. You don't know who it was, but I'm supposed to, right?"

"Isn't that what you're here for, Deputy?"

"You know as well as I do that I'm here to serve papers an' stuff like that. There hasn't been a murder down at this end of the park since Willis Johnson chopped his old lady up with an ax, and that's been almost fifteen years ago."

I started to speak but he held his hand up to cut me off. "I know," he said wearily. "I know what you're going to say. I'm talking about murder, not hanging. Let's not get into that again just now."

"Fine, we'll quarrel about definitions some other time. The fact is, it was only poor shooting that prevented another murder last night."

Jack grunted. "You can prove that, of course."

"What?"

"I said, you can prove that, can't you? That you really were shot at, I mean. You have witnesses?"

"You know I don't. I was riding alone. Just me and the horse, and he's a closemouthed scutter. Why don't you ask the murderer instead?"

"You are being unreasonable, Cyrus," he said with exaggerated patience. "In the first place, there is no murderer. You're sitting right here beside me, healthy as a hound dog, which means no murder has been done. If someone had found your body lying in the road, *then* we would have a murderer to go looking for."

"So just because he's a lousy shot . . ."

"Shut up, Cyrus. I'm trying to explain this to you. That was in the first place. In the second, I've got only your word that anything happened at all. Like I said, you're sitting here with not a scratch on you to show that anything happened. You don't have another soul to say they saw or heard a thing last night. Even by your own account the worst thing that really happened to you was that you lost some sleep last night. Cyrus, that just *isn't* enough to start a manhunt over."

"I'm not asking you for a manhunt. Just an investigation."

"Same thing," he said, "just a matter of degree."

"And you won't do it."

"That's what I'm trying to tell you, dammit. There's nothing I *can* do. I have no knowledge that a crime was committed, Tetlow. Nothing but your word. That isn't much."

"Especially with you, right?" In the darkness I could faintly see his shoulders rise and fall. "I still want to make a complaint about it," I insisted.

"Consider it complained about."

"A formal one," I said.

"All right," Jack said slowly. "In the morning, which is not very damned far away now, I will sit down and with my very own hands write out a complaint report. Is that better?"

"Much."

"Why?"

"Because if it happened once it might happen again. If it

does, I'm shooting back the next time. I want it on record *why* I would."

"Looka here, Tetlow, if you go shooting any citizens I, personally, will haul you up to Fairplay and jug you for it. And that's a fact."

"You mean it's all right for them to shoot at me but not for me to shoot back."

"That isn't what I said at all, boy, but you'd better know it. If you shoot somebody, you're mine. And you'd better thank me for it if it happens. Otherwise you might end up like your pa and your big brother, Tetlow. Now you think about *that,* why don't you."

"Attaboy, Jack. You keep giving the people that kind of justice an' you'll be sheriff yourself someday."

"I intend to be," he said seriously. "Right now, though, I'm tired of listening to your sass. I'm also just plain tired. I want to go back to bed. Are you quite done now?"

"No," I said curtly. "The reason I came into town yesterday was to see you. I want to find out what's happening with my other complaints."

"This was a pretty nice job until you came back," Jack grumbled.

"I don't intend to leave for the sake of your convenience."

"Pick whatever reason you like," he said. "One way or another, though, I expect to see you leave." He cleared his throat and added, "You might still be able to swing that exchange. Poor land for good cattle."

I ignored that and said, "My complaints, Jack. My sworn and legal complaints. What about them?"

"I investigated them, of course. That's my job, see. No one knows anything about an alleged hanging five years ago. No one but you *says* they saw any bodies, even."

"I buried them myse—"

"Shut up, dammit. Like I said, there's no evidence that a crime took place. That's exactly what I reported to the sheriff. The investigation is closed for lack of evidence. As for the other thing, George Ryal had Sunday dinner with us." From the tone of his voice I didn't have to be able to see his face to know he was enjoying being able to twist that knife. "I asked

George about the fence and the bull. He says the fence is on his property and was his to cut. You're welcome to prove otherwise but you'll have to hire a surveyor to do it. He also says he doesn't know anything about your bull. You can hire a lawyer and file suit if you like, but that would be a civil matter for recovery of damages. None of my business. I checked on that, too. So do it if you want. It'd be your word against his."

"By golly, Jack, there's one thing I've got to say about you. You're consistent. Totally, absolutely, completely consistent. Not worth a damn, of course, but reliable about it."

"Get out of my sight, Tetlow. I'm going back to bed." He stepped down out of the buggy and made his way carefully back toward the house. I sat there impotently hoping he at least would get rock cuts on his feet. That seemed about the most I could hope from the evening.

After a minute or so, I crawled down myself and went toward where I'd hidden my horse. I didn't want to be anywhere close to town or the public roads come dawn, and first light was coming near. It was already clear that I really would not like a fugitive's life.

CHAPTER 18

I'd come by way of Kester, which is certainly the long way around, but while there I'd dropped a letter into the storefront mailing slot. I wanted to keep old Amos Gordon informed. And if that makes it sound as though I didn't fully trust Deputy Jack Delaney, well, that is only because it's so.

Anyway, I didn't want to ride home the same way I'd come, and I certainly did not want to take the usual road homeward, so I turned my horse east and hoped I would fool the fellow Jack would not admit existed.

You know, it is a funny sort of thing—odd, that is; I sure wouldn't laugh at anything that might save my life—but now that I had need of it, I was beginning to remember some of the things I'd heard when I was little. Things like that business of not going back to a place by the same route you used in leaving it. That way if someone saw you going and found himself a place to ambush you on your way back, he could wait there until he grew roots and put out spring buds without getting his crack at you.

That and maybe a few other useful tricks I had learned without really knowing I was learning anything. At the time I'd just been having a good time listening to the grown-ups yarn.

The park had been settled and peaceable for an awfully long time now. Like I said, I myself had never heard a shot fired at a human being until that one was fired at me. But that same thing could not be said about all, or even about very many, of the men who'd come in here to settle or about the men before them who came to work their places and left when the free gold played out. It sure as the devil couldn't be

said about the really old-timers, the ones who came here back
in the '20s and '30s to trap.

Of course, for all I heard about those old mountainmen, I
never actually met any of them. I guess they were mostly
gone before I was ever born.

I sure used to enjoy listening to the exciting war stories and
Indian tales, though, when the grown folks talked. Most of
them had been through the big war back east, and some of
them had taken part in Indian fights. Some said too that the
Saylor brothers, Cletus and Monroe, had been involved in the
Lincoln County War down in New Mexico. They never spoke
of any fighting down there except against Apaches but I'd always liked best to hear their stories. I guess I kept hoping
they would tell about Billy the Kid, but they never mentioned
him on their own. In fact, the only time I heard them mention
him at all was once when they were asked outright, and the
only thing they said then was that he hadn't been near so famous live as he was dead.

Anyhow, from listening to them and the others, I had
learned a lot more than I realized at the time.

I cut east and a little south to avoid the public road and by
dawn was across the grass and back to the timbered hillsides.
I hunkered down in the protection of a thick rock spire at the
back of John Bluick's land and gave some thought to my situation while I ate a cold breakfast.

I suppose I could have just climbed up higher and spent the
day hiding on Bluick's summer range, but the truth is that I
just plain wanted to go home. It wasn't only that I needed to
keep an eye on the house and my livestock. The most of it was
that I wanted to be home, to be on my own place even if it
meant traveling in daylight to get there. I *felt* better at home.

The thing is, though, I could travel up in the timber only so
far. Much of the way, sure, but there is a lot of straight up
and down rock in those mountains that neither horse nor man
can negotiate. So I started out anyway, telling myself I was
probably nine kinds of an idiot for doing it but wanting to
anyhow. Maybe I'd have been better off giving in to my ex-
haustion and sleeping the day through.

I rode high and I rode careful, dipping down toward the

flat basin only when I had no choice and getting back up again as quickly as I could. It was hard on the horse but that was his tough luck. I was already so tired my head felt like it had been overfilled with green slime and was about to burst.

By late morning I was near the upper end of the Ryal place. There was timber cover all the rest of the way now and I was close to home. I guess what with one thing and another I let my guard down.

I crossed onto Ryal's place. And the truth is that unlike the other fences I had crossed I didn't stop to repair the gap behind me. He hadn't bothered fixing mine, so why should I trouble myself over his fence.

The timber was pretty solid here and I rode deeper and deeper in my saddle.

I came to a narrow chute, just a shallow little dip that wouldn't have been noticeable except that it was clear of any sizable tree growth. Above it there was a granite face that was just inclined enough to hold snow, and below it was a jackstraw tangle of rotting logs. It didn't take much to figure out that it was a snowslide that had cleared the chute. The wonder was not that it had happened, but that under those conditions there had been enough time between big slides for any trees to grow as large as those down below me.

I was riding along dumb and happy like that, thinking about snowslides, and it being summertime, when for the second time I heard the sound of a bullet sizzling past my ears and soon behind it the sound of the shot itself.

Oh, Lord. Not again. But I sure was awake now.

I lay down against the bay gelding's neck and laid the steel to him. He shot out across that open area like he was just as anxious as I was to clear it. His speed was quickened all the more by some flying rock chips as another slug struck the ground in front of him and went whining off up the chute.

We reached the pines and plunged into their protection.

This time I wasn't running for home, though. I snatched the bay down onto his haunches in a sliding stop. Before he was halted, I had my carbine in my hand and was down and running. Running back toward that treeless chute.

The shots had come from downslope. That was just fine. I'd

always heard the war vets say that holding the high ground was the biggest part of a victory. I bellied down to the dirt and crawled the last little way to the tree line.

Below me the tangle of snow-broken logs offered all the hiding places a murderer could ever wish for. I lay with the old gun in my hands and tried to search each and every one of the thousand places he might possibly have chosen.

The shooting had wakened me but that was past now. The slow, incessant searching dragged at my eyelids. After several long minutes I realized that I had been moving my eyes, but I hadn't been seeing anything. The inspection had become a mechanical thing, and nothing that I was seeing was registering in my brain. I could have been looking straight at him and I wouldn't have known it.

I tried to go back and start over, but it was no good. I began nodding over the sights of my rifle. By then he could have been two miles away anyhow. I gave it up and went back to my horse. Thank goodness he had stayed ground-tied. A lot of them won't no matter how hard you train them.

I said the heck with the sharpshooter. As soon as I was back on my own land, I found a place to hole up and crawled into it. If anything needed my attention, it could just wait. I was going to sleep.

CHAPTER 19

I'd already suspected that a fugitive's life is a lousy one. I was right. Laying up in the brush while some rifle-carrying fool looks for you is less than great.

I spent three days that way, moving each night to a new spot and spending the daylight hours curled up on top of a rock where I could watch the country below without being seen. As far as I could tell there wasn't a soul anywhere on the place besides me. No one bothered the horses in the little trap. The cattle I couldn't see because of the folds in the ground, but I didn't see anyone going to or from where I thought they would be.

The third evening, shortly before dark, I saw a person come up the road in a light rig. Whoever it was was alone and driving a vehicle right out in plain sight. There wasn't any hiding about it.

What was more, shortly after he disappeared inside my house the lamps were lighted and the shutters opened. It became kind of difficult to sit there and watch the lamp-glow from my own place.

I debated on it, but after a while decided to go on down and see who it was. If this was a sucker play, it was working.

Scar was saddled and I guess was about as bored as I was, for even after so much rest he never offered to crowhop the first time when I climbed onto him.

The trip down to the house took nearly two hours and would have been a lot longer if I hadn't trusted the horse so much. The lights were still showing when I got there, and the buggy horse was standing hitched in the yard.

I left my horse tied behind the cistern, made sure my rifle was ready, and slipped up to the back wall afoot.

"Do you want to come inside or should I come out there?"

I recognized the voice right away. It was the Sorensan girl.

"Am I *that* clumsy?" I asked through the open window.

"It wasn't real loud but I could hear you coming," she said. "I take it you'd rather I come out?"

"If you don't mind."

I heard the scrape of a chair on the floor and a few seconds later the lamps began going out. When it was dark I heard the front door close, and she came around toward the back where I was waiting. She was right. It was too, too easy to hear the soft crunch of footsteps on the gravelly soil. She came around the corner to where I could see her and motioned me over there.

"Could we at least sit down somewhere? I've been on my feet all day."

"Sure."

"Would the buggy be all right?"

I followed her to it and handed her up the step. She settled onto the padded seat with a relieved sigh. I walked around the rig and climbed up beside her. After so long sitting on the ground or sprawled over rock I had to agree. It was comfortable.

"This feels kinda familiar," I told her.

"I borrowed it from Laura. It's her dad's."

"Does she know . . . ?"

"Where I wanted to go? No. She knows I like to get away to relax in the evenings sometimes. And to tell you the truth, I'm not sure they would have let me use it if I told them why I wanted it."

I grinned. "It's been a long time since my name was welcomed in that house."

"Well, it's less welcome now than it had been."

"That's hard to imagine. Now what?"

"You've been writing some letters. Jack doesn't like that. Neither does Mr. Delaney."

"Did the sheriff get after him to do something about my complaints?"

I heard a low, throaty sound that might have been a

chuckle. "Don't get your hopes up, Cyrus. Nothing that drastic."

"Yeah, well, that figures. What did he say then?"

"Nothing that would please you, really. Just some mild curiosity. He wondered when he would have some reports in case he has to answer any questions about it."

"You're right, that isn't much. I'm surprised the Delaneys are upset about it."

I could see her shoulders rise and fall in a slight shrug. "Anything said is too much as far as they're concerned. They just wish you would go away and let the park forget the name Tetlow."

"That won't happen," I told her.

"I know it. They do too, really."

"What about Laura?"

"Oh, she knows it all right."

"But is that what she wants, too, now? For me to just go away?"

"I really couldn't say, Cy. I don't think she knows for sure herself."

"She's still seeing Ryal, though?"

"Yes. He came in twice this past week to see her. George is a very welcome guest with the whole family."

That figured. Mrs. Delaney was one of those warm and genuinely nice people who sees the best in everyone and likes them. The men of the family would accept *any*one as a suitor for Laura so long as his name wasn't Cy Tetlow. And of course young Ryal had everything to offer for Laura herself. I reminded myself that that once-upon-a-time interest had been decided some days ago anyway. I wasn't supposed to care any longer.

"Is that what you drove all this way to tell me?" I asked, perhaps ungraciously.

"Partly," she said. "And I wanted to ask you something, too. From what Laura has said you told Jack and wrote to the sheriff that someone took a shot at you. Is that true?"

"Yes. It was true the first time I told Jack about it. And they tried again three days ago when I was on my way home from seeing him that night. In fact, the first time it happened I was on my way back from trying to see him."

"Was it the same person both times?"

"I wouldn't know," I told her. "I didn't see him either time. Whoever it is is pretty good at staying hidden."

"It sounds like you suspect Jack might have done it himself," she said.

"I guess it's possible it could have been coincidence. If I have any suspicions, they sure aren't enough for me to put in writing. I can't prove much of what I think, and I still don't want to be sued for saying more than I could defend in a court of law."

"But you do believe it?"

I smiled. "I never said that."

"My, you *are* being cautious, aren't you?"

"Not as much as you might think, Beth. I really didn't see who did it, and I'm not much for going off half-cocked. I'm fairly patient." I grinned. "Scared half to death but still patient."

"Has it been very bad?" she asked with the concern apparent in her voice. It was nice to hear, and if I'd known her better I would have thanked her for it. Maybe I should have anyway, but I wasn't much used to having people be friendly. I had about forgotten how to handle it.

"Aw, not too bad, I suppose. I don't use the house anymore, and I've spent my share of time outdoors before."

"Am I placing you in danger by asking you to sit out in the open here?"

"If I could answer that, I'd know an awful lot more than I do now."

"Cy, if I did anything to harm you, or to cause it, why I'd just *die*."

I laughed. "Let's hope not."

"Oh, God. That was stupid of me, wasn't it? I mean, you really *could* die if I led a murderer to you." There was a quaver in her voice.

"Hey, calm down, girl. Nothing that serious has happened yet. If I'm lucky—and careful—nothing will. Okay?"

"That's nice of you, Cy, but I just couldn't keep you out

here another minute. Look, I may want to get in touch with you again. How could I do that and not . . . expose you?"

"Give me a minute to think about that." I wanted a cigarette awful bad while I was pondering her question, but I just didn't dare light one out here in the open. "You could leave me a note easy enough. Not in the house. That wouldn't be safe. You could leave it, like, on the woodcutting block behind the house. I wouldn't want to come back and check there every day; so if you do, you could leave a shutter open on a back window. If you come at night, open the shutter and leave a lamp burning. I'll close all the shutters before I leave tonight. If I see one open, I'll know you've been here."

"All right, but I'll close the shutters. You go on, Cy. I'll close things up here."

I nodded and climbed down from the wagon, my carbine ready. If anyone was watching they would wait to shoot until I was clear, I was sure. "Beth. Thanks for taking the trouble. I really do appreciate it."

"You're a nice man, Cy. I think you're carrying a heavier load than you've earned." She sighed. "Go on now."

I began to fade off toward the shadows, preoccupied now, wondering if I again would see the yellow flare of a muzzle flash.

"Cy."

I stopped and crouched low to the ground.

"Good luck, Cy."

I went on, feeling not nearly so lonely now as I had been.

CHAPTER 20

You know, I had never spent much time thinking about what it means to be able to just sit and talk to people in a friendly way. Until I knew there was somebody wanting to kill me, I guess I'd never really thought about it at all. Now, though, just those few minutes talking with Beth Sorensan seemed a very rare and special privilege.

I didn't just lay around and think about nothing but that sort of thing, of course. My cattle needed some looking after, few of them though there were, and I had to do that after dark. During the day I had to keep an eye on the place so I could try and figure out who or even how many were after me. But I did have plenty of time on my hands, and a body has to think about something when he's looking out over a piece of empty grass waiting for something to move on it.

When I was a kid I'd always had friends and so didn't think about the having of them. Later, I'd gone through a period when I had hated every man, woman, and infant in the whole park. The hating had been enough for me then, I guess, and I hadn't needed friends or thought I didn't.

When I went outside to work that first winter and the winters thereafter, I found it easy enough to be with people and talk to them and get along. The times in between, when I was home in the park, it was only temporary and didn't seem to matter much. Those were mostly waiting times anyway.

Now it seemed different somehow. Maybe it was because the waiting time was over now or maybe it was just the man with the busy rifle, I wouldn't know which. Whatever, I was more and more beginning to feel that, if I was ever going to accomplish anything here, it would have to be this summer or I wouldn't get it done at all.

And in a way now, maybe I was more afraid of winning than of losing.

If I lost I'd be run out of the park, out to where I was the same as everybody else. Where I'd be judged for myself and not on what people thought of my family. Where I'd already proven I could make it.

If I won, though, I'd be staying here in the park. Where people would learn to hate me for showing them to themselves once they learned they were wrong about Pop and Kyle. Where my own land would be like an island in a sea of hard-set faces and not a true friend among them. Where I didn't truly know if I could make a go of things, it having taken the three of us and all we had to offer to make it pay before.

And either of those possibilities was just in the event that I would live long enough to win or to lose.

Any of the three could come to pass and in due time I would find out which. In the meantime I had to keep trying. If I didn't try it would be the same as saying I didn't believe in Pop; and if I didn't have that, then I didn't have anything.

Which, if nothing else, can all be put together as an example of how muddled and muddied up a man can get when he has too much time on his hands and too many thoughts roaming loose in his head.

I was out of coffee, which was bad, and I was about out of tobacco, which was worse. There wasn't much choice about it. Go get or go without.

I wasn't about to be making any purchases at Delaney's store, and I didn't want to be gone long enough to ride all the way up to Fairplay, so I saddled the little dun and headed over west to Kester.

I got there before daylight and laid out in the brush until the store opened. When it did, I was the first customer through the door.

"Morning, Tetlow."

"Good morning, Mr. Goodson."

"You come by for your mail?"

"No, sir. I just need a few things."

"Suit yourself." He took out his pocketknife and used it to shave a generous chew from one of the plugs in his display case. He shoved it into his mouth and grunted his satisfaction with the taste. It would have been his first of the day, for I'd heard him complain often enough that his wife wouldn't let liquor or weed either one into the house. He spat an almost clear stream into the sand bucket he kept by the counter and said, "The government says I got to offer it. They don't say you got to take it."

"Sir?"

"Mail, boy. I said you got some mail here."

I shook my head. "Nobody knows I come here."

"Somebody does," he said.

"Have you told anybody?"

He snorted a bit of profanity past his chew. "I don't owe you anything, Tetlow. If anybody asks me, I'll tell him. The only reason I haven't is that nobody's asked." I wished I could tell if he was lying. "Some reason I shouldn't say anything?"

"Somebody's trying to shoot me is why."

If I was expecting sympathy from him, it was stupid of me. He spat another stream, darker this time, and said, "You're just lucky they missed you the first go-round."

Oh well, that sort of thing didn't bother me much anymore. "I'll take a sack of coffee, already ground. A half-dozen pokes of makings and papers to go with them. A couple cans of peaches. And my mail."

He grunted and turned away.

"Wait. Some stamps too, I think. A half dozen of them." If I came here again it would be at night, to the mail drop not the store.

I paid for my purchases—it took most of a dollar for those few things—stuck the sealed-and-stamped envelope in my pocket and got out of there before I might decide to get mad. I'd thought I really was long since over that, but apparently I was not. Not completely.

I turned the dun toward the timber and moved him out of there fast.

CHAPTER 21

I headed down country a way before I felt safe enough to cross the coach road down toward Salida and climb up into a place where I thought I couldn't be found. Hoped I couldn't, anyway.

The dun deserved better than to be made to stand with a tight cinch, but I couldn't afford to give him the relief. There wouldn't be time to tighten it if I had to move off in a hurry, so I let him stand and found myself a protected niche where I could watch my back trail. Only then did I take the time to pull out the letter.

There was one sheet, written with a pen. It said:

"Cyrus, Rec'd yours of recent date. Find it hard to believe men of this park would murder. I would like to talk to you about this."

It was signed by Amos Gordon.

Well, I wasn't totally amazed. Mr. Gordon was a nice man, but he had also found it hard to believe that anyone would have hanged Pop and my brother. His difficulties hadn't made that any less of a fact either.

If anything about it surprised me, it was that he wanted to talk to me about it. The note definitely said that it was Mr. Gordon, not the sheriff, who wanted to talk.

But all right, I decided. If he wanted to talk, we'd talk. I was already out away from home and apparently hadn't been spotted. If I was going anyway, I could save myself some riding by going straight up there. I swung back aboard the dun and got him started.

By the time I got up to Fairplay, after skulking nearly the entire length of the park, it was late afternoon but Gordon was still at his desk in the sheriff's office. It looked like everyone else had gone home.

"Good evenin', boy. That was sure fast. I didn't expect to see you for a week or better. Just mailed my letter the day before yesterday." He didn't try to lift his bulk from the chair but waved me to a seat near him. "You weren't carrying a rifle the last time I saw you."

"No, sir. I didn't need it the last time."

"You sound serious, boy. You want to tell me about it?"

"I'd like to ask a question first."

He took his pipe off the desk and spent maybe more time than necessary getting it going. "All right," he said.

"Where'd you hear I could get mail at Kester?"

He laughed and looked much more relaxed than he had a minute before. "That's easy, son. Postmark. Your letter was postmarked there. I figured if you'd been there once, you'd be there again. Took the chance on it anyhow. If you stop by the hotel down home, you'll find another just like it. Ignore it if you come across it sometime."

I guess I relaxed some too. "You haven't told anyone else?"

"No cause to. If you'd like, I'll shut up about it even if there is cause."

"I'd like."

"All right, then. That's settled. Now tell me about this shooting business."

"It's a long story without much of an ending," I said.

He puffed on his pipe and said, "Take as long as you like. I'm in no hurry."

So I told him. All of it that I knew but little of what I suspected. Mr. Gordon hadn't gone stupid, though, for all the white on his head and bulk around his waistline.

His pipe came to the end of the tobacco with a wet rattle, and he knocked the hot dottle into a spittoon beside his chair. He cocked one eye at me and said, "Your voice sounded a little different when you were saying you'd been to see our deputy. D'you know that?"

I shook my head.

"It's a fact." He fiddled with the empty pipe. "If I wasn't sitting in this office, if I was just an old friend, say, what would you tell me about what you *think*, Cy? You gave me the facts. What do you think?"

Again he got the head shake. "I've talked to some people about the laws, Mr. Gordon. That could be called slander if I can't prove it. Well, I can't prove it."

"Where'd you study law?" he asked with a smile.

I grinned back at him. "Leadville some. More down at the Springs last winter."

"You did it deliberate?"

"Uh huh."

"You wouldn't make a bad deputy, son," he said casually. His attention came back from wherever it had been. "Did your, uh, advisors mention that anything that remains in confidence is safe to say?"

"I don't remember anything about that. I guess I never considered it a possibility."

"It's a possibility," he said.

"What it is, is a risk," I told him.

"Your decision, of course." He waved a hand. "Ah hell, forget it. I know what you'd tell me anyway, I figure. No need to put it in words. Look here, Cyrus, how long has it been since you've had a good, solid, sit-down meal behind your buckle?"

"It's been a while," I admitted.

"Then you'd better join me over at Winman's. It's as good a meal as there is this side of Denver. My treat." He climbed heavily out of his chair and tucked his glasses away in a coat pocket. "Come on, son."

"I can't hardly turn down an offer like that."

We ate, Mr. Gordon putting away a lot less than I expected of a man his size, and he was right. It was a fine meal. The best I'd had since I came back to the park.

We didn't talk about anything important. Little, gossipy things about people we both knew. The usual appraisal of grass and water conditions and the probable beef market trend come fall. He knew more about it than I expected and never once brought up minerals.

Of course he knew as well as anyone how cow raisers feel about hardrockers, but still it was thoughtful of him.

By the time we left the restaurant I was pretty comfortable

with him and likely would have told him my suspicions if he had asked.

It was just as well that he didn't ask.

Not ten minutes after I left Amos Gordon, where I'd been summoned by his request, some son of a bitch was laying up in the grass and tried for me again. And this time he was shooting better.

CHAPTER 22

I don't know if my new habit of sharp vigilance (funny how that word can change meaning so much when you just use it different) was paying off or if I was just lucky. Whichever, I heard a soft click off to my right that sounded very much like a rifle being cocked.

It could have been any one of maybe a thousand things, but I wasn't taking any chances. I laid the steel to the dun and jumped him out of there at just about the same time as I saw the muzzle flash.

I should have been a half second quicker, though. The bullet cut across the back of my shoulders like a bullwhip being laid onto me.

It hurt like fire—quite literally like fire—but I could tell right away that it wasn't a solid hit. I stretched out along the horse's neck for a few jumps but just long enough for me to haul my carbine free. As soon as it was in my hand I dropped off of him and hit the ground rolling.

This time I wasn't going to make it easy for him. This time I figured to fight back.

The dun bolted out of sight in the darkness, and within moments the night was quiet.

I slithered around on my belly until I was facing toward where I thought the shot had come from. I was hoping he would have been able to see me come off the horse and would think he had nailed me good.

My shoulders hurt like crazy now, but there wasn't time to pay attention to that yet. Getting that lousy ambusher was more important.

I lay there and tried to control my breathing. The .44-40, nearly as old as me, lay ready in my hands.

The insects and toads or whatever got over their scare and began their assorted chirps and whirs and croakings again. Pretty soon that stretch of dark, empty grass was as noisy as your average city street, though in a much nicer way I would have to say.

Anyway, it began to get pretty loud, which meant that if he was still there he was being as cautious as I was. I kept on waiting.

A few minutes more and the bugs shut up again. *I* sure wasn't moving, so he had to be.

I'll say one thing for him. He was good. I never did hear him coming, and it was sheer luck that I caught a thin reflection of starlight on a buckle or gun or something.

It was too dark to aim good but I sure could point. I leveled my carbine and cut loose of one. The muzzle blast was enough to blind both of us.

When I could see again, I cranked a couple more shots through the rifle in the general direction of where he'd been but down around ground level.

As soon as I'd fired I rolled fast to my left, feeling like I'd left my back stuck to the ground behind me when I rolled on it, but the effort was wasted. He didn't shoot again.

I lay there for what seemed like a long time, blinking and staring and wishing I could see in the dark.

At least this time, though, I wasn't as deep-cold scared as I'd been before. At least this time I could shoot back, and if he came for me again he wouldn't get me free for nothing.

After a time, fifteen minutes or maybe longer, I heard the creak of saddle leather. It couldn't have been from more than fifty yards away. I heard that and then the sound of a horse jumping off into a hard run.

The sound faded quickly and after it did I felt alone out there. I don't know how to explain that, exactly. I hadn't been able to see or hear a thing more before that than I could now, but now it *felt* different. Nothing I could put my finger on about it. Just different.

I sat up, carefully now as I was all of a sudden really conscious of the pain in my back, and let the hammer of my carbine down to the safety notch.

I hadn't noticed it before but the night air was kind of cold on my back. The bullet had sliced across the cloth as slick as a sheepherder's knife. By a little judicious touching and twitching, I discovered it had sliced across the skin over both shoulder blades just as neat.

The two wounds—there was a gap between them since my shoulders stuck back a bit further than at the spine—didn't seem to be bleeding much. It was more like they were draining with a slow ooze. Not that that made them feel any better.

Something else that made me feel no better at all was realizing that if that bullet had flown a quarter of a damned inch to the side from where it did, it would have clipped the spine. And that would've been all there was to one Cyrus Tetlow.

I saw a fellow in the mines once when I was mucking. He was a powder monkey shooting a stope up along the vein. Whoever had been handling the pry bar on the last shift had missed a chunk of loose rock in the ceiling. When the powder monkey, his name was Geniella, a Portugee I think, bent over to pack the drillers' holes, that rock dropped down on his back.

The chunk weighed maybe twenty-five or thirty pounds and wasn't particularly jagged or sharp. It didn't even break the skin where it hit him, but I guess it hit just wrong. He went down like somebody'd placed a shotgun to his forehead and pulled the trigger.

Oh, he wasn't dead. But he wished he was. He never moved or felt another thing from his neck down, and the company doctor said he never would. The doc didn't seem concerned about it either. I guess he'd seen such things before.

They packed the powder monkey off to some state hospital, and I guess he'll be there until he quits breathing.

I sure wouldn't want to spend my days like that. I know for a fact I'd rather take one in the head than in the spine.

Anyway, the wounds themselves were hurtful and annoying, but really nothing worse than that.

I stood up and looked around and had another thought.

I hadn't any idea where my horse was.

He wouldn't have gone too far. He would be somewhere within a mile of where I stood, probably within a half mile.

But where? There wasn't any way for me to tell without looking and it was sure too dark to see.

I sighed and let my rifle slip down until the butt was on the ground. There had to be some bushes or trees around here where I could hole up.

And that was all right. I could use the rest.

CHAPTER 23

The dun found me before I ever started looking for him. Some time during the night he drifted back to where I was stretched out sleeping. He was there when I woke up in the morning. Of course a horse can use scent about as well as your average dog, but still it surprised me.

I sat up, forgetting those shallow gouges across my shoulders, and paid the price for my forgetfulness. It hurt like crazy. More, actually, than it had the night before.

I cussed and grumbled some, but there wasn't anybody around to offer sympathy except for the horse and if he felt any of it for me he never showed it.

As usual these days I had some food in my saddlebags and, since it was coming full light anyway, I stayed where I was long enough to have some breakfast and boil a pot of coffee.

A wagonload of laughing boys—men I maybe should call them, at least half of them looked as old as I am—drove by while I was eating. They called out and waved and invited me to join them. I shook my head, but in a way I wished I could. They looked pretty carefree.

I knew what they would be. A hay crew, no doubt arrived on the late train last night and being picked up early this morning by the fellow they'd hired out to for the summer.

Up at this end of the park where there was so much water, they cut a lot of hay and shipped it out on the cars to Denver. There was always a market for it there because of all the stable-kept city animals—drafters and light harness and some saddlers. A fellow with land good enough for cutting hay didn't ever have to be broke.

Anyway, these boys were enjoying themselves and it started

my day off nice to see them. I waved back to them and watched them out of sight.

I finished my coffee and kicked the fire apart. I almost hated to resaddle the little dun horse so soon. The only time the thing had been off him in well over twenty-four hours was while I ate, and that wasn't good.

The sun was already up over the east wall by then, and I wasn't going to be able to hide from anybody here. It was a long way to the timber, and the last time I'd taken that route I was shot at. I decided what the heck, I might as well go straight home this time. That probably would be the *last* thing my ambushing friend would expect.

It occurred to me then, though, that, for no really good reason, I had been insisting to myself right along that I was dealing with just one person doing the shooting. Oh, I had mulled over all sorts of possibilities in my mind, but the truth was that I'd really been thinking in terms of just one person.

Yet this last attempt happened halfway across the park from where people might have cause to be afraid of me. As best I could guess, the vigilance committee crowd had all come from the south end of the park.

No one up here would likely want to shoot me. Yet no one man could cover the whole park with ambushes and hope to get near me so often. *No*body could be that lucky. And even I couldn't be that *un*lucky.

So it was possible that the whole of that old vigilance crowd had decided to protect themselves by doing much the same with me as they had the rest of the family.

There was one other possibility, I realized. Three times I had been shot at now. And each of these times I'd been out in public to see the law. Twice to see Jack Delaney. And now to see Amos Gordon. At Amos Gordon's request, at that.

The fact was, too, that five years earlier it was the same Amos Gordon who hadn't done a thing to bring those committee men to answer for killing my father and brother.

No matter how nice he'd been last night—at the same time as someone was waiting to take another crack at me, by golly —for all I knew, Amos Gordon had been riding with that crowd five years ago. They sure couldn't have gotten any trial evidence against Pop and Kyle, Jr. Maybe that was Mr. Gordon's private way of enforcing justice in the park.

Now *that* was an interesting possibility for sure.

I wasn't a hundred percent positive that I bought it. Not yet. But I had to consider it.

It was certainly easy to believe it of Jack Delaney. And if one deputy, why not another?

And I could believe it as well of the others, the ones who had done the hanging. They had killed two Tetlows already. Maybe they'd just gone and set some sort of minimum-age requirement before their good-citizen consciences would allow them to make a clean sweep of it. And I really was a threat to them now. At least I darn sure hoped that I was. I was trying my very best to be one.

I thought about that, over and over again—about each person who might be involved and each group of people who might be—time after time while I rode the tough little dun horse south through the park.

I was worried at first about another ambush, but I was riding slowly while I did my thinking and pretty soon the three-times-a-week hack from Fairplay down to the Springs came up behind me in a boil of dust.

The light rockaway was going at a fancy clip with only one passenger and a mail sack to weight it down besides the driver. I touched the dun into a lope to hang beside them.

"Mind if I ride along?" I called over to the driver.

"Public road," he answered. He looked me over like he'd never seen another like me and asked, "What for, mister?"

"I been sick," I told him. "If I black out, I'd like to know there's somebody near." I hated to lie to the man, but I'd have hated worse to tell him the truth, which was that I figured an ambusher was much less likely to shoot if there were witnesses about.

For one thing the truth sounded awfully melodramatic. For another, any good driver would put the safety of his passenger and coach above that of some stranger. He just might balk at the idea of exposing his rig to even the remotest chance of trouble.

So I handed the man a bald-faced lie and used him for an

escort the rest of the way down to the crossroads. The whole way there he kept looking over to make sure I was all right, though he never said anything and seemed to be trying not to be obvious about it. I thanked him when we got there, but he waved it aside. "Forget it," was all he said.

The hack changed teams there, and I wished I could do the same. The dun had been hard used the past couple days and couldn't keep up with them on the eastward run. Another ten miles and he'd be done for, and then where would I be. Maybe in trouble.

I'd hit on the idea of using other people and public places to protect myself, though, and now that I'd started it seemed a pretty good idea.

I was already in town; and even if that was the hornet's nest, it seemed a safer place for me right then than open country would be. Especially until I could let the dun get rested.

I bought the horse a sack of oats at Delaney's. Laura wasn't behind the counter and Mr. Delaney and I managed to complete the transaction without either of us having to say a word. The atmosphere in there was not exactly friendly.

Normally I'd have sacked out again at Smitty's, but his shop was closed. Probably he'd finished a job for someone getting ready to mow hay—rakes and cutting bars always seem to be needing work done to them—and was drinking up his income over at Garrigan's place.

Which pretty much ruled that out as a waiting place too.

Smitty tried hard to be nasty and obnoxious when he was sober, but he didn't do a very good job of it. When he was drunk, and even Mr. Garrigan had given up trying to keep him from it, he managed genuine nastiness quite nicely. I didn't want to be around him then.

So I left the horse tied in the shade and decided to just wander around for a few hours.

Without particularly planning on it I found myself drifting over toward the schoolhouse where Beth Sorensan taught.

CHAPTER 24

I certainly had no intention of going inside or of disrupting the school day, but when I came in sight of the building I found the school kids playing out in the yard.

Some of them, the little ones, were playing, anyway. A few of the older ones looked to be big enough louts that I wouldn't want to fight them more than one at a time. Those boys weren't playing but were hunkered down in a close circle like so many conspirators planning a jailbreak, and I wondered how Beth could handle them. And, for that matter, why they'd be in school when there were hay crews making up.

Anyway, I figured it wouldn't hurt to shuffle in closer since I wouldn't be disturbing anything now.

The bigger boys, old enough to know who I was and to've picked up some notions from their fathers, gave me some cold looks, but the little ones eyed the carbine I was carrying and looked big-eyed and envious. They were the ones of an age to be excitable and probably more than a little disappointed that the Wild West wasn't so wild as their daddies' stories made it out to be. Personally I was wishing it was a lot tamer than I was finding it lately. My back still hurt plenty, and at that I was lucky.

Beth was standing in the shade of the big cottonwood beside the schoolhouse, keeping half an eye on the kids and talking to someone I couldn't see behind the much-carved old tree trunk. My initials were on there too somewhere, I remembered now.

I wandered over that way, telling myself it would only be polite to say hello now that I was here.

Laura Delaney was the person standing on the other side of that tree.

Darn, but I felt egg-on-the-face foolish all of a sudden. I hadn't been prepared to see Laura here and didn't know what to say to her now that I had.

I needn't have worried about that.

Laura looked at me like I was a bug on the kitchen counter. It was very much the same sort of look her father had given me just a few minutes earlier. That had never happened to me before—not from her it hadn't—and it hit me kinda hard.

Laura's chin came up until she was actually, not just a figure of speech but quite actually, looking down her nose at me. Still staring right at me she told Beth, "I'll talk to you later, Bethy. When we won't be interrupted."

She gathered her skirts and swept past me as grandly as any lady in Denver could have done it. I couldn't help but turn my back on poor, plain Beth to watch while Laura marched away in the direction of the Delaney house.

When I finally remembered my manners and turned back to Beth, I pulled my hat off and tried to force a smile. I intended to say something polite by way of a hello, but Beth had kind of a shocked look on her face.

"Cy! What happened to your back? Your short is torn and that looks like dried blood on it."

"Oh." For a minute there I had forgotten about that. "I, uh . . . it was a bullet did it. Last night. It's just kind of like a burn, though. Not serious really."

If she was upset by that piece of information she didn't much show it, although she did seem to be concerned.

"It will have to be cleaned up," she said calmly. "It might get infected."

"I'll wash it up when I get a chance," I assured her.

She gave me a critical look and said, "You can't even reach it there. I don't see what good you could do yourself. You stand right where you are, Cyrus, and let me handle this." She wasn't taking any no for an answer, either.

Beth turned toward a group of older girls clustered at the side of the building. "Sarah Wren."

"Yes, ma'am?" It was the oldest-looking of the three girls who answered.

"I'm dismissing you all early this afternoon," Beth said. "I

want you to tell everyone and get them started home, Sarah
Wren. Mind the little ones don't forget their lunch pails."

"Yes'm," the girl said happily. She didn't wait for further
explanation but hustled off about her business.

"Is that Sarah Wren Stone?" I asked.

Beth nodded.

I shook my head. "I remember her and her folks, but she
was this high then."

The schoolteacher laughed. "I've only been here a year and
already I can see them changing. And you're stalling. You
come with me, mister." She led the way to the front steps and
on into the classroom.

It was different now than it had been for the dance, the big
teacher's desk back where it belonged at the front of the room
and all the chairs and writing desks in rows the way I remembered them from so long before.

The kids rushed in, in a shoe-slapping hurry, and rushed
back out again with their empty lunch pails and whatever else
they had brought with them. The place was quite a mess
when they were gone.

"No after-school chores today," I said. "I'll help you with
the chalkboard and stuff."

"You will *not*," she said firmly. "What you will do is sit
yourself in that front row and be patient. I keep a few things
here for the children's cuts and scrapes. My hydrogen perox-
ide should work just as well on you."

I did as I was told and waited while she got a flat metal box
from a drawer in her desk. She stood over me and ordered,
"Shirt off, please."

"Yes, ma'am." It was easy enough now to see how she con-
trolled those big lummoxes who made up her upper grades.
The woman just didn't leave any room for disagreement.

I peeled out of my shirt and sat still while she swabbed
some high-smelling stuff onto the two scrapes. It smelled
worse than it was, though. It felt cold but didn't hurt.

"No, don't move yet," she told me. "I want to wrap that so
you don't get dirt in it."

"It's too high up. You can't wrap that without wrapping me
all over."

She looked me over from a couple angles and finally grunted. "I guess you would look like a mummy at that. Be careful of it, anyway."

"I will," I promised. I started to reach for my shirt but she stopped me.

"Not yet," she said. "The children get embarrassing rips in their britches sometimes too." She put the medicine box back where it belonged and got out a sewing kit. She sat behind her desk and began stitching over the bullet holes in the back of my shirt.

"I'm sorry about what happened outside," she said without looking up from her needlework. "Jack is still awfully upset with you, and the things people are saying about you these days aren't very nice. I think George has been telling her things, too."

"Yeah, well, I guess that's to be expected. It's all right, really." I managed a grin and added, "As long as I know I've been straight with everybody it can't get too bad. Besides, it's better in the long run if she does favor Ryal's side of it. He can do a whole lot more for her than I ever could."

"You really are a total idiot, aren't you?"

"Thank you, ma'am."

"Any time. You deserve it well enough." She bit the thread off and put her sewing gear away. "There. Wash that and it will be as good as new almost."

"That's mighty kind of you."

She shrugged the thanks away as if she hadn't hardly heard or hadn't wanted to and said, "It may all be seen in a little different light when you report this shooting, Cy. No one could pretend that you made this up. Or that you did it yourself. This they'll have to believe."

"Huh!" I shook my head. "There isn't much point in reporting this. That just might be the *worst* thing I could do, in fact."

She left the big desk and moved to the chair closest to mine. "Tell me what you mean by that."

And I did, taking my time about it and kind of going over it again in my own mind while I was doing it.

I told her about the different possibilities and how I kept

coming back to Jack Delaney and now maybe Amos Gordon, too. That might have been a mistake as she was Laura's best friend and so close to the rest of the family, but once I got started talking I never thought to tell myself to shut up.

"It's a problem isn't it, Cy," she said when I was finally done.

I grinned. "I think you could say that it is, for a fact. I can't get anything done about Pop or about my place without the law's help. And the way it stands right now I'm scared to go to the law again. Neat, huh?"

"Really." She handed back my shirt and I pulled it on, feeling some better after I did.

"Cy, have you thought about going up to Denver? Maybe the Attorney General's office . . ."

The truth was that I never had thought about anything like that, but I was sure willing to consider it. Beth cut that short herself, though.

"No," she said, "that wouldn't work either. They would just check with the sheriff here. So that wouldn't change anything." She sighed. "If I could think of anything, do anything. . . ."

"Thanks, Beth, but look, don't worry about it. You've done plenty this afternoon just by being so nice about everything an' so helpful. I really appreciate that. And I'd best get out of here now before I give you even more of a bad name. You don't deserve that."

"I wish I could . . ."

"Don't worry about it, I told you. Really. It'll work out." I wished I really believed that. I stood and picked up my carbine. "You've been swell, Beth. Thank you."

I pulled my hat on and got out of there, not really sure if I should feel better or worse for the afternoon's conversation. But it was awfully nice being able to *talk* to someone. And the more I was around her the more I enjoyed Beth Sorensan's company in particular.

CHAPTER 25

My back felt a whole lot better now, and in truth I think that might have had more to do with the fact that somebody had cared enough to tend it than with the benefits of the tending itself. Anyway I was feeling pretty good again.

It was still way too early to leave town. The dun horse hadn't had enough rest yet, and it was too long until dark. Of course the darkness hadn't exactly given me much protection so far, but it sure felt safer and I preferred it. And it was still true that a man couldn't draw a fine rifle sight by moonlight.

If there was anything certain now, it was that I was not welcome at the Delaney house, and Smitty's place wouldn't be fit for another human to enter until tomorrow or maybe longer. I decided to kill the time by treating myself to one of the big, full-course, dollar dinners they served at the hotel.

The only local people in the place were the ones who worked there, so I laid my dollar down and really enjoyed myself.

Afterward, I got into a pleasant conversation with a couple travelers, one a bob-wire salesman from Illinois state and the other a geologist from Delaware looking for work with the first mining company he could hook on with. I gave the geologist the names of a few people I knew up in Leadville, and the three of us made a pleasant evening of it. I hadn't come to town for pleasure, but I had had plenty of it before I left.

The dun was feeling better for the stop too. I watered him at the public trough and set him onto the road for home.

It should have been obvious to anyone who might have been watching that I would follow the road out of sight and then duck off so I couldn't be found or followed—obvious to anyone thinking in terms of an ambush, anyhow—so I did what I hoped was the unexpected and took that road all the way home at a quick and comfortable road jog. I was glad to get there too. It felt like a long time that I'd been gone.

I laid up in the rocks for several days and would have been pretty darn comfortable, really, except for my back itching all the time. Not that I should have been complaining, considering what more that bullet could have done to me, but I cheerfully ignored my own good advice on that subject and complained anyway.

That peaceful time lasted only so long, though, and late one afternoon I saw a pair of riders come down the road, straight down to the house. They turned their animals loose in my corral and left them there in plain sight, so they sure weren't trying to hide themselves.

I sat in a little nest of gray rock and watched. One of them chopped wood and carried it inside while the other tended the animals. Even as far away as I was I could hear the ax strokes rising to me through the thin, clear air. I could see tho fall of the ax and a little while later I would hear the strike. Whoever it was set a fast pace and soon had his work done. Both of them disappeared inside, and a few minutes later I saw smoke coming thick from the chimney.

They spent tho night in my house and made free use of my coal oil for most of it. There was no way that anyone in sight could not know the place was occupied.

Come morning, they kept their smoke going long after it should have been needed just for cooking purposes. After a time they carried chairs out into the yard and sat themselves down in plain sight. I began to get the idea that they wanted to have a talk and weren't going to go away until they got it.

All right, I decided. I'd go see.

I went down on foot, thinking a man can hide where a horse would be given away, taking only my carbine and lots of time. I tried to sneak down like a wild Indian, and I guess it worked. I stepped around the corner of the house with a ·44-caliber muzzle leveled at thom and they both jumped like I'd just squalled into their ears. They nodded a welcome once they had their composure back, but they didn't try to pretend it was a friendly welcome.

I knew them, of course. Monroe Saylor was one of them. A man named Harold Wyke the other. They both ran cattle in the park and both generally went along with what other men decided. Neither was much of a leader, a thing I figured I should keep in mind. Whatever they were here for, it likely was not their own idea.

"Good morning, gentlemen."

"We aren't armed," Saylor said.

They both spread their arms and stood up. They turned around slowly. If they were carrying pistols or even knives, they were well hidden.

"I take it you want something?"

"Uh huh. We want to talk."

"No trouble," Wyke said. "Just a talk."

"All right."

They got up again and started toward me.

"You can talk from over there," I told them.

"It'd be more comfortable up close," Saylor said.

"I'll be more comfortable if you stay there."

They didn't appear to exactly like that but they sat back down.

"Now what is it you want to talk about?" I still had the gun on them.

"You," Saylor said. "You and your future."

Maybe he wanted me to get into the conversation there, but I waited him out. He could have his say without my help.

"Yes, well . . ." He started to rise, I guessed so he might be able to pace and think. This wouldn't be going the way he would have pictured it. He thought better of the movement, though, and stayed where he was.

"You're wasting my time," I prompted.

"Okay," he said quickly. "The Delaney boy made you an offer." He paused again.

"I wasn't interested. I'm still not. If that's what you came about, you're wasting your own time too."

"No," Wyke said. He glanced at Saylor, obviously wanting him to do the talking.

"What he told you about," Saylor said, "there's more. A little bank account to help you get started, carry you through the first year like."

"You can stop right there, gentlemen. You really are wasting my time." I began to back away around the corner but Wyke stopped me.

"Boy? We've been hearing it around that somebody shot at you."

"I suppose you wouldn't know anything about that," I said just as sarcastically as I could.

"God's truth, boy. We don't. We're honest men, Tetlow. We wouldn't hold with shooting a man down."

I gave him a bitter grin. "Hanging maybe but no shooting, huh? Not you. Well I happen to know better, Mr. Wyke. I'm the one being shot at. And in a way I regard that higher than I do your bribery. At least whoever is doing the shooting thinks enough of me to know I won't be bought like some steer in the market pens. Now get out of here and don't set foot in my house or on my property again."

I turned my back on them and walked away in plain sight of them both. If they'd had guns on them, they could have shot me easy but right then I wouldn't give them that much credit for nerve. And I guess I was right.

CHAPTER 26

I had another visitor down at the house a few days later. I was almost beginning to feel popular, by golly.

This time, though, the visitor was a welcome one. I knew who it had to be right away because in the morning when I checked over the place I could see that a shutter had been left open, and a horse wearing a sidesaddle was tied out behind the shed again. It had to be Beth.

I rode down there, cautiously but not expecting trouble beyond my normal expectations of it lately. Which was enough. When I got there, the smoke was rolling from the chimney. I left my horse beside hers and went inside.

It was Beth all right. She was at the stove cooking something.

"Hello." The way she said it, we might have been in town and I might have been a normal visitor dropping by to pay a social call.

"Hello yourself. Are you about done with the fire?"

"Almost. Why?"

"It might not be a good idea to advertise that the place is being used. Someone might want to come see who it is."

"I hadn't thought of that, Cy. Sorry." She began pulling the fire, drenching the coals in a bucket of water she must have carried in herself, for I did not remember leaving one inside. "There should be enough heat left in the iron to finish what I'm doing here anyway. Except maybe for the coffee. If it's weak, don't fuss at me about it."

"That's a deal," I said.

I took a seat at the table, and pretty soon she had a meal down between us. Damn but that was the best-tasting stuff I had had since I couldn't remember when. I don't know if it was her cooking or my hunger that made it so, but it tasted even better to me than that meal I'd had with Amos Gordon the evening I was shot. I told her so, and she seemed pleased by the compliment.

"You haven't said why you came," I mentioned while we were cleaning up the dishes afterward.

"I . . . the truth is that I've been worried about you. I wanted to see how you're doing. That's all, I'm afraid. I don't have any good news to deliver."

For some reason that touched me more than any news or warnings or direct help could have done. I mean, that was just plain *nice* of her. Just plain nice.

The dishes were all done and we settled at the table with coffee.

"Could I ask you something, Beth?"

"Of course."

"You've been so . . . nice to me, the way no one has for as long as I can remember, and I appreciate it. I mean, I really do appreciate it. Yet about all I know about you is that you're a friend of Laura's and you teach school in town. That isn't very much when you think about it."

She shrugged and for the first time, at least the first time I had ever seen, she looked a trifle embarrassed. "There isn't that much to tell."

"I can't believe that. And I really would like to know. I mean, it isn't like you *owe* me any explanations or anything. Lord knows you've done more than I could ever ask or even hope for. But I would like to know more about you."

She really did look to be embarrassed now that the conversation was directed toward her instead of toward me and my problems the way it always had been when I was around her. She was a funny kind of girl in a lot of ways. I decided to wait her out for an answer, give her a minute to get over her shyness if that is what it was.

After a little while, say half a cup of coffee's worth of time, she dropped her eyes away from mine and began to talk in a low, soft voice.

"There honestly is not that much to tell you, Cy. I'm just . . . a nobody from no place interesting."

"I can't believe that, Beth."

She gave a short, bitter little laugh. "But it really is true, you see. It really is." She glanced up briefly and then down again. "I'm twenty-two years old, Cy, and I never in my life have ever done anything . . . special, or exciting, or interesting.

"I grew up in a little farming town in Iowa. Cyrus, have you ever *seen* a little farming town in Iowa? No? Of course not. Well believe me, Cy. There is nothing, I mean nothing as dull and as unexciting as a little farming town in Iowa. My parents are nice, ordinary, unexciting people. Pot roast every Sunday. Vegetable soup every Wednesday. Everything very nice. Very dull.

"I went to school and made good marks. I graduated high school and went to normal school. I went back home and lived with my parents and taught grade school. There isn't much else for a homely girl to do in Iowa, you see. I sang in the choir. I read a lot. I learned to play the flute." She looked up and gave me a sad little smile. "How many people do you know who can play the flute? Well, I can." She paused, and I think she was remembering something.

"Last year it all began to seem so . . . so infinitely boring somehow. I could look forward to all the endless years ahead, and I knew they would all be exactly the same, my pupils would be the same, everything would be exactly the same except the dates on my reports and on my letters. If I had anyone to write letters to, which I didn't. So I . . . decided it was time I should become my own person. If I was ever going to do that, it was time that I did it. Almost anything would have been an improvement.

"I wrote to the registrar at the normal school and asked for a list of school districts that might need teachers. They sent me some suggestions, and I looked up the places on a map in the school atlas. Most of the schools were in Iowa, of course. I didn't look up any of them.

"There were two in Colorado. They sounded . . . foreign and far away. Cowboys and wild Indians and all that. I looked them up. One was in Pueblo. This one I couldn't find on any map anywhere in my home town. That is what made my decision for me. If it wasn't on the maps, it just had to be in the wildest and woolliest part of everything I had always heard about the West. So I wrote them and sent an application, and I was hired by mail and I got on the train, which was the first time I had ever been more than fifty miles from home, and now here I am. End of story."

"I don't think so."

"Really. That's all there is to it. Or ever has been."

I shook my head. "No, I don't think so. Somewhere along the line, Beth Sorensan, you became quite a nice person yourself. Sorry. Maybe you don't like that word, but it fits. A bright person too. I know I'm no kind of a character reference, especially around here, but I like you, Beth Sorensan. You're a very nice person, and I like you. And I very much appreciate your friendship."

Darned if she didn't begin to cry, although I sure God never meant any of that to be an insult. I got up and made something of a production out of filling the coffee cups again, which drained the pot. I hoped I didn't need to distract myself again because I wasn't sure what I could have done the next time.

"I'm sorry," Beth said after a minute or so.

"Yeah, well, I don't want to bring it on again. But for what it's worth, I meant every word of it."

She smiled. Sort of. "Well, I like you too. I told you once before, Cyrus Tetlow. You're one hell of a man. It's just a lousy shame things have gone the way they have for you."

"Everybody has problems."

"Tell me about it," she said with the bitterness heavy in her voice. Somehow I could not quite figure why a nice girl like that should feel so kindly toward everyone else in the world and so harshly toward herself.

We dropped the subject, anyway, and talked some more about things that were not serious, and after a time I slipped away and went back to my hiding places on the mountain. But I had enjoyed, I mean *really* enjoyed, visiting with her for that time. It had been very special to me, and I was grateful for having had it. And I found that I genuinely had meant the things I had told her. Beth Sorensan seemed to be a genuinely nice girl and a good one beneath her plain looks.

CHAPTER 27

It was kind of lonely up there, especially so after the visit, but I really didn't know where else to go or what else to do. The law didn't seem to be doing me any good, and about every time I showed up among people somebody took a shot at me. It seemed fair to assume that I was not popular here.

There wasn't even any work for me to keep busy doing. With so few cattle and so much grass—well, so much in relation to those few head of beeves, anyway—all I had to do for them was to leave them alone so the good high-country grass could work inside them.

The situation with the horses was the same. The horse trap had enough grass to carry twenty head through the summer, but there were only two head in there now.

So I sat up on the rocks that I now knew even better than when I was a kid, and I kept a watch over the emptiness below me. I kept one or another of the using horses saddled beside me, but I hadn't anywhere to go on them.

The first hint I got that there was something starting to happen was about a week after Beth visited. I began to hear riders moving on the lower slopes in the night, several of them at a time, and there were tracks showing higher and higher on the mountain.

After three nights of that, they found my horses except for the one I had saddled as a night horse, which happened to be dependable old Scar. The rest they ran off with a great amount of hollered cursing and crackling brush and nighttime confusion. I could hear them easy enough, but I wasn't close enough to see anything or I would have thrown some shots their way.

Judging from noise alone I might have guessed there were a

dozen of them, but the voices sorted that down to a more likely three or four. I tried but I couldn't make out any kind of guess from the voices about who they were. None of them really sounded familiar, although there was one I thought I had heard before but couldn't place.

Come morning, I was mad and more than a little bit worried. If someone had taken to running off stock, as they had, it meant they were getting plenty serious. More serious in a way than shooting at me had been, for a man might sometimes decide to settle his affairs with a gun and still be understood if not exactly forgiven. But stealing horses goes beyond any hope of either understanding or forgiveness. It sets the thief at a level below manhood. It is a thing that just is not done. Usually. Like any other, that one is a rule that everyone believes in when applied to the other guy even if he doesn't always live the belief himself.

And like I said, I was mad too. Probably because I was scared. It was one thing for me to be shot at. I could fight back about that. But if there was one place where I was really vulnerable it was with my livestock. There just wasn't any way I could guard them all the time. If someone wanted to run them off or just shoot them all down, I didn't see how I could stop them.

They could hurt me that way. Bad. Everything I'd worked for, for the past five years, was tied up in the few dozen cattle grazing down on the flat. They were my future or what hope for it I had. My few heifer calves each spring built up my small herd however slowly they did it, but it was the steers that made it all work.

Those few steers I was able to sell each fall allowed me to pay the taxes on the land that was the base of it all. Without them, I just didn't know if I could make it.

I worked every winter but I sure couldn't always count on finding something as cushy as that caretaker's job had been. Every winter I had to support myself in town while I laid aside enough to support me through the warm months too and hopefully have a couple dollars left to buy a heifer or three.

Now I already had to find a way to replace my bull. If I

had to take on the taxes and a complete herd replacement too, I just didn't know if I could do it. I might go under, all the way under.

So I was deep-down scared and was mad at whoever was doing this; and while I knew there was no way I could possibly protect my cattle, I knew I had to try.

I saddled Scar and began working my way down the mountain.

There were two men sitting horseback beneath a rock outcropping. I'd been riding above them, just about to make my way around it and down to where they were.

I'd heard their voices—at least I didn't have to worry about giving myself away that way—and left Scar and bellied out onto the rock to see. It was a sharp drop down there and I was practically over their heads.

One of them was George Ryal, Jr., so it looked like he'd joined the pack and would fit right in with the rest of the vigilance-minded gentlemen of South Park.

The other was a man I hadn't seen before. It was hard to tell from such an unusual angle, but he looked to be in his thirties or forties. He could have been another new rancher himself or maybe just a trusted hand from any of the ranches big enough to hire permanent help. Thieving was not the sort of work you would trust to itinerant seasonal help, it was sure.

". . . up here somewhere," I caught after I stopped moving so the sound of cloth dragging over stone wasn't drowning them out any more. I was pretty high up, so Ryal's voice wasn't loud though it was clear.

"We've covered it pretty thorough," the other man said.

"Dammit!" Ryal barked. "If we'd covered it that thorough, we'd have found him. So don't give me that crap. We just haven't looked hard enough."

"Or high enough. He might be ten miles back an' over on the next mountain somewhere," the man I didn't know said.

Ryal shook his head firmly. "No way, Mickey. No, sir. Those horses were no higher than this, so neither was he. It's all that night-riding made us miss him. You can't find a camp at night if he doesn't keep a fire, and he doesn't. That is obviously by now."

"But . . ."

"I know," Ryal cut in. "I know. You told me often enough. It's safer if he can't see us. Well dammit, we can't see him either. From now on we do our looking in the daytime, like it or not. And we do it until we find him. And the first one who does see him better shoot the son of a bitch dead. And that *better* be before the twentieth."

The other man grunted and began building himself a cigarette. Me, I got to doing some thinking.

According to what Ryal just said they were after me hard and heavy, and they had a deadline for getting the job done. The twentieth day of the month.

Why? For that matter, when? I hadn't the least idea what day of the month this one was or the twentieth would be. And I sure had no idea why they would want me grassed before then. Ryal sounded like he had a sure enough reason, but I couldn't imagine what that reason could be. It was a mystery to me plain and simple.

I laid there thinking about it and squirming around on that rock, which wasn't too comfortable anyway. That might have been all right, I suppose, except that I got stupid about it. My wallowing around shifted some loose rocks on top of that outcropping and sent a couple of them skittering over the damned edge.

They hit close enough to spook the horses below me and they *sure* got the attention of those fellows.

Ryal looked up and I found myself looking him eye to eye. He began to color up with anger.

Whoever the fellow was that was with him, he wasn't slow. The man had a pistol in his hand even before he had his horse under control, and the next thing I knew there was the loud, hollow boom of a big-bore handgun and a greasy streak of lead showed up like a bright silver chalkmark on the rock about four feet from me. It was a darn good thing the man wasn't as accurate as he was fast.

The man's horse didn't seem to be used to being shot off of.

It was already buggered, and it really blew up now so that the fellow had his hands pretty well full.

Ryal's mount was back under control, and George cussed me some and cussed his partner some and began hauling his saddle carbine out of the scabbard.

My own gun was already pointed in his direction in a general sort of way and I suppose I should have knocked him off his horse. It would have been easy enough right then.

The truth is I thought about it. My impulse was to pull the trigger and settle at least some of my problems right there.

I thought about it but I just couldn't do it. Part of that was because of Laura. She seemed to have decided on George Ryal, Jr., for her future, and I didn't want to do anything to hurt her.

The other part was that that was a human being down there below me. And maybe he wanted me downed, but all I really wanted of him was a replacement bull and to be left alone.

I guess I just wasn't ready to actually send a bullet into another man's chest. Not yet. I triggered a shot into the gravel under his horse's belly and began scrambling backward across that rock.

CHAPTER 28

They were coming after me, Ryal and that rider and however many more I couldn't know, but I did know there were more.

I wasn't much more than out of their sight when I heard a string of three quick shots, a pause and another string of three. That is a "come here" signal in any man's language.

They were coming and I was sure going.

I leaped down off that rock and snatched up Scar's reins while I was already on my way up into the saddle.

There was no going downhill now the way I had planned to do for they seemed to be spread out below me, and it is hard for a horse to make time running uphill. It is hard for them anyplace and at nine or ten thousand feet high it's that much worse. The only good thing about it was that ugly old Scar was mountain bred and mountain true. And their horses would have to go even harder if they were going to catch up with us.

I headed back up the way I'd just come, and I hoped there wasn't anyone in this crowd who knew the country well up here.

Of course they wouldn't need to know it too well. Once they found the way up to where I'd been, up above that weathered knob of rock, they could track me pretty much at a dead run. The ground up there is not so much soil in the way a flatlander thinks of soil, you know, fine dirt or clay or sand, as it is a loose, grainy gravel. An animal walking soft, especially on the flatter parts, will leave darn little of a track behind it and a man none at all if he is careful of his bootheels.

But an animal that is running or is climbing will leave dark scrapes where the sun-dried top layer has been disturbed, and it stands out as plain as fresh ink on paper. They could track me sure.

I pushed the bay gelding hard to where I'd had my last camp and swung off him long enough to grab up the flour sack I kept some food in. I didn't figure to be back here for a while.

From there I figured I had to take a chance on letting them close on me and hold my horse down to a walk in the hope he wouldn't leave any readable prints until he had to do some serious climbing again.

Ryal's friend had had a pretty good idea a while ago. I was heading as far up and as far back as I could get. There wasn't much of anything between me and Cripple Creek except rock and trees and some leftover snow fields. It was country where a man could get far away from people and I expected to do exactly that.

A quarter mile was all I could manage without having to climb.

It wasn't much of a gap between tracks but if I was lucky maybe it would do. I had to hope so.

The horse scrambled up a chute that would have been carrying water a couple months earlier. Now it was dry enough that a flatlander probably wouldn't have known what it was. That was good. It meant I was still a long way from the snow you could nearly always see above the park late into July or even August. Some years it never left.

Anyway, there was no way up without climbing and leaving tracks, so I climbed and left tracks.

The quakies were fully leafed out now but not so many of them. From here up it would mostly be the dark spruces and firs. None of the peaks right around here got much above timber line, though I could look across the park to the west and see enough of them that were bald.

There was an easy, gentle glade rising above the chute and curving off to the left. It looked entirely too easy and too logical, so I turned toward the right. That was the way to the high empty.

I rode south by east, always higher and always deeper into the mountains. Whenever possible I took to bare rock, wish-

ing when I did that I could pull Scar's shoes but not willing to
chance his hooves barefooted for as long as I might need him.
The brown mare was miles away now. The rest were gone.
For that matter, the mare and old Nero might be gone now
too. Depending on them would have been sheer wishful
thinking, so I just had to put up with the metal scrapes I
might leave on the rock behind me.

Several hours of that and I began to feel safer. I hadn't seen
or heard a thing from the men who had been chasing me.
They might never have seen my tracks going up that chute.
They might have followed that glade leading north and eventually back down toward the Wilkerson Pass road. Maybe. I
kept riding.

I stopped for lunch well after noon. I didn't need the rest so
much as the horse did. I hadn't been moving him fast but it
had been uphill and steady.

I didn't dare light a fire, of course, or pull the saddle, but at
least I could get off his back and let him browse for whatever
edible wisps he might find.

I thought about taking the food sack and trying to put together a cold meal, but that was pointless. I knew what was in
it. Dried beans. Coffee. A little rice. Bacon. The thought of
raw bacon makes me gag and the other stuff would have to be
cooked too. I left the sack where it was and sat in the sun
with my rifle across my knees.

It was warm in the sunshine, though it was pretty nippy in
the shade. The warmth felt good. Any other time I probably
would have slid down and put my hat over my eyes and let
the sounds of Scar's chewing lull me to sleep. Instead, I sat
there and tried to stay alert while lack of sleep pulled at my
eyelids.

To the north, down the way I'd come a half hour or so before, a pair of mulie does got up from their bed and hit a
loose-legged trot downslope and across into some timber
below where I was sitting.

I enjoyed watching them and was wishing I had some field
glasses so I could see them better. I've taken my share of them
for the meat, but I enjoy just watching them as much as I do
hunting them. It would have been a long shot down to where

they were, but I could have taken either of them and it was nice to know that.

I was paying too much attention to those does, I suppose, and wasn't thinking about what might have gotten them off the bed when they'd lain quiet while I passed.

Scar coughed. That is what it sounded like, anyway. Just like a cough as the breath was driven out of him.

A couple seconds later I heard the shot. It was funny but it was like the horse had been waiting to hear it so he would know what was happening. As soon as the sound arrived, his knees buckled and he slipped down.

He lunged up again and managed a dozen leaps that carried him down the hill away from me before he went down for good.

They rode out into view then, out of the timber where those does had been bedded. There were three of them, six or maybe seven hundred yards away.

It was too far away but I wasn't reluctant about it anymore. I aimed at the center one of the three, holding about two feet over his head, and triggered my rifle.

The bullet missed but it came close enough to worry them.

They all wheeled their horses and broke back into the cover. I threw another into the trees for good measure and began clawing my way straight up the slope behind me. Since I didn't have a horse anymore, I might as well run where horses couldn't follow.

On the exposed slope below was the dead horse, still wearing my saddle and nearly everything I owned, including my food. Right now, though, that didn't mean a thing to me.

CHAPTER 29

If I wasn't at timber line I was quite close enough to it, for I was out of cover except for the bare, jagged rock. The soil here, what there was of it, was coarse and jagged and quick to slide. What it came down to was that I had run just about as far as I was going to be able to.

Directly above me was a sheer rock face. To the north, at my back the way I was now sitting, was a stairstep series of ledges and faces that a man could climb like a ladder if he happened to be fifty feet tall or better, otherwise it would take ropes to get down; and I don't know of anything that could have gotten a person up higher unless it might be those wedge and ring gadgets the eastern tourists liked to use climbing for sport on the rocks down at Garden of the Gods.

Ahead of me was an open slope bare of anything except the spill of sharp gravel that formed it. I couldn't really go that way either, for it was unlikely that I could cross it. Movement on loose gravel that steep was almost certain to mean a sliding fall that would be wilder than any toboggan run I'd ever made as a kid.

So I wasn't planning on going anywhere.

I settled down beneath an overhung niche in the cold, gray rock and I waited, my carbine in my lap and as ready as my five remaining cartridges would allow. The rest of my ammunition was still in my saddlebags, attached to a dead horse a mile or so to the north and maybe two thousand feet lower than where I went to ground.

The rock was cold and as soon as I quit moving so was I. It was past noon, and my side of the peak was in deep shade. Up this high it is pretty cold all year anyway, and whipping wind didn't make it any better. I had my vest on but no coat—

it was tied behind the cantle of my saddle—and I was wishing for a lot more.

As if I needed a reminder there was a dark clot of discolored, dust-covered ice lying at the back of the overhang where I sat, collected there where the rock and gravel met. For the past half hour I'd been skirting crusted patches of old snow in the areas protected from direct sun. There was a lot more of it up higher. I could smell it on the wind.

Even if Ryal and his friends turned and left now, I wouldn't be in a comfortable situation, and so far they hadn't shown signs of going anywhere except after me.

Twice I had caught glimpses of them climbing afoot behind me. Each time I saw only Ryal and the one he'd been talking to when this whole thing started. That pretty much meant that two of them had come after me, I figured. The third should be waiting and watching in case I tried to circle back somehow and reach their horses or the supplies still on Scar.

I hadn't seen them lately, though, and I was hoping they had lost the trail. It was possible they had though much of my running had been uphill climbing where even a man leaves clear gouge marks in the gravel.

And I was right. It was too improbable to hope for. They hadn't lost me.

I could hear them coming, mostly the thin, sliding trickle of small gravel falls as they climbed. They weren't talking now, though. They wouldn't have breath to spare for words now, I knew.

One nice thing, breathing hard from the labor of fast climbing they wouldn't be able to hold a rifle really steady. At least I had the benefit of a few minutes' rest, and that might make a difference.

They came into sight finally, below me and to the left at a distance of several hundred yards. They climbed atop a flat jut of rock and stopped to get their breath and look around.

I could have shot either of them in that moment, and maybe I really should have. What stopped me this time wasn't any humanitarian ideas—I couldn't afford such now—but the hope that if I stayed quiet they might pass me by and think I had gotten down that steep ladder off to the left. Two men could probably make it down there, I thought, and they might believe I had done it. If so, I might be able to slip back down the way I'd come up and get an advantage on them. I knew good and well, though, that if I shot one now the other would be out of sight before I could lever and fire again, and one man who knew where I was could keep me penned into my hole until help arrived. He couldn't get to me, I didn't think, but I couldn't get out either.

So I sat where I was, as motionless as I could be without dying.

It was that darn Ryal who sat down and did some studying before they moved again. And worse luck, he had some field glasses with him, which I didn't see until it was too late.

I don't know if it was my footprints that pointed him toward the overhang or what, but before I realized what he was up to and might flatten myself against the ground, he had his glasses on me and was looking straight at me.

I made a vulgar gesture at him and raised my rifle. By the time I had it to my shoulder, Ryal and his friend were down and out of my sight.

All right, I figured, we had ourselves a standoff. They couldn't get to me, and I couldn't get out to them.

So I was stuck right where I was at least until dark when I could make a try across that gravel slope. Even if I took a ride down to the bottom of it then, it would be better than getting myself shot.

And things could have been worse. I was cold it was true but, shucks, if I got really thirsty I could chip some of that ice behind me. I still had my pocketknife anyway.

And, boy, was I right. Not only could things be worse than I figured, they already were.

An old-timey gunfighter or a proper outlaw probably would have realized it first thing and never put himself into the situation I had, but I hadn't exactly been raised to think that way.

Anyhow, the rock that I thought was protecting me turned out to be just perfect for splashing bullets off of, which Ryal didn't seem to have any trouble grasping.

I was halfway stretched out there on the gravel and the next thing I knew there was this loud, vibrating *kwang* and a bullet thumped into the ground not more than six inches from my right boot.

There was a brief pause and another one hit the ceiling. It struck the rock more straight on than the first one and most of it lodged there—I could see it stuck there in a flattened lump—but a few pieces splattered around me. I never felt any of those bits hit me, but I began to feel something trickling down my forehead. I brushed it aside and my fingers came away red and sticky. I seemed to be bleeding a little from the scalp and it was probably a darn good thing I'd had my hat on to help slow the fragments.

The rifle fired again, and a bullet whined nastily into the ice at the back of my hidey-hole.

Judging from the interval between shots, there was one of them firing while the other stood ready for me to bolt out of cover.

And it was going to work, too. If I stayed under that overhang, they were going to chop me up into small pieces one little bit at a time. I hadn't any choice but to move and as soon as I did they would have their clean shot at me.

It didn't take a lot of planning to know what I had to do. There was no good way higher but forty or so yards away there was a fast route down. I'd just have to hit that gravel and ride it down as far as it wanted to take me. If I was risking a broken leg, that was still better than staying.

The rifleman fired again and I didn't wait to see where that one hit. As soon as I heard it splash on the ceiling, I leaped up and out of there so at least one of the rifles would have to be levered before it could fire again.

I came up fast with my carbine in my hands and threw a wild shot downhill in the general direction of where I'd last seen them. I hadn't any hope that it would do more than distract them, and if it did that much good I wouldn't know about it.

The one who'd been waiting for me fired before I had taken three steps and he must have hurried his shot. The bullet struck behind me and threw gravel that I could feel against my boots and pantlegs.

I ran low and hard for that loose gravel slide. One of them fired again. I heard the shot but not the bullet.

I reached the end of the hard ground and flung myself out toward the top of the slide.

I was already in the air when I felt the bullet hit. It was much like being hit with a huge mallet, a curiously dull but very deep sensation that I heard as much as I felt.

After that I was dimly aware of motion and of the smell of dust in my nose and of a kind of cloudiness. For a while then, I don't think I was aware of anything at all.

CHAPTER 30

I was wedged into a crevice or sort of crawl space underneath a boulder that had fallen from somewhere above and was leaning against the live rock of the mountain face. The pain was starting to come to me now, but right at the moment I was more aware of my shivering and the clatter of chattering teeth than the wound.

I vaguely remembered being at the foot of the slide area—if I remembered correctly that would have been four hundred feet or so below where I'd started—and crawling upward to try to get away. After that things were kind of hazy.

Now I was aware of things again though in a detached and somewhat uncaring way. One of the things I was aware of now was the sound of voices. Two men talking. I knew they were hunting me. I really didn't care.

They were saying something about looking for a blood trail, finding some on the rocks where I'd ended up but nothing after that.

That was easy enough to figure out. I'd been shot at the side of my back, on the left side. The wound would have been staunched by all the dust and grit thrown up by my side. I landed on my back so I left blood there. When I crawled away, the wound was off the ground and not bleeding enough to drip on the ground.

Simple. I felt highly superior to be able to figure that out when they couldn't. Had one of them asked me, I would have explained it to them. I gloated to myself some and was tempted to call out to them so they would come and I could tell them how bright I was. I was tempted and might have done it except I didn't have that much energy.

Nothing really hurt all that bad, though. That was nice. I

knew there was pain but I was too far gone to feel it very
much. I mean, I *knew* it. But I couldn't exactly feel it.
It was kind of like the voices. I knew what and who they
were. I knew what the words meant. I just didn't care enough
to make those separate word meanings come together and
apply to anything.

I smiled a little and cradled my head on my arm and, still
feeling very bright and very superior, I took a little nap.

The next time I came awake it was dark and much, much
colder. I began to move, wanting to huddle in on myself in
search of warmth, but that was a mistake.

A fiercely hot wave of pain tore a scream out of my throat,
and my agony was redoubled with the thought that Ryal and
his friends would have heard.

I lay shivering from the bitter cold and at the same time
running icy sweat in anticipation of their coming. For one
brief instant there, I forgot about the pain that kept washing
through me.

It was almost worth the fear for that one moment of forgetfulness. At least my mind was clear now. I remembered my
first wakening, recalling it with amazement and relief that I
had not given myself away. I could have done that very easily, would have done it if I'd had the energy to call out, and
now I would have been dead. Now I would have been feeling
nothing.

That in itself was almost a temptation. To be able to feel
nothing at all seemed the ultimate bliss. Surely nothing could
be above that. Surely nothing could be below what I was feeling now. Nothing.

I thought I had known pain before. I've been kicked by a
cow and thrown by a fair number of horses. I've been thrown
around by giant-powder blasts underground and had the
usual boyhood collection of minor disasters and a couple of
broken bones.

None of that was remotely related to this.

The bullet had gone into my side well toward the back and
now was lodged somewhere inside me.

I've seen bullets from similar rifles blow clear through a

two-hundred-fifty-pound buck and pass nearly through a half-ton bull elk, but this one hadn't gone through me. How deep it penetrated and where it went inside me, I had no way of guessing but there was certainly no exit wound. I must have been lucky. Perhaps not too oddly I didn't feel at all lucky just then.

Still, I did think about it some. Maybe the cartridge had been undercharged or the powder old or the cap weak. Maybe the human body is just a whole lot tougher than I ever would have guessed. I have no experience to judge that. The fact was, though, that I was still alive.

There were times during that night when that was in doubt. There were times too when I came near to regretting that I was there to feel it all. The lure of nonfeeling was very strong.

But not *that* strong.

After a time I began to wonder which was the worse, the gunshot or the cold. Either of them alone would have been agony. Together they were unbelievable.

I waited for days for that one night to end. Each bone-deep thrust of the cold made me shiver. Each shiver disturbed my wound. Each tightening of my muscles in response to that pain seemed to allow another thrust of the cold into me. It went on like that and on again in a cycle that seemed to have no end.

Eventually my eyes began to hurt too and I realized I was beginning to be able to see the shape of the rock that surrounded me.

That was encouraging for some reason. I had survived the night, and I guess that really was reason for encouragement.

Later I began to see color too, somber gray and black changing slowly to pale flesh that had been gray and mottled gray rock that had been black.

Ahead of me, deep in the gap between boulder and wall where I lay hidden, was another trapped bulge of milky-white ice. From where I lay, unable to touch it, it looked soft. The edges were rounded from the small amount of melting that had taken place, and it was no longer touching the boulder, although its contours were matched to the stone.

Looking at it—and I certainly had nothing else to look at—

made me realize how thirsty I was. It seemed a long time since I'd had anything to drink, and it had been nearly a full day. I'd lost blood since then too. I'd heard that you needed to drink a lot if you'd been bleeding. I began to believe that was good advice.

I forgot about my thirst then. I heard voices and the crunch of footsteps on gravel.

Ryal and his friends were back.

CHAPTER 31

There were three of them there now. Either someone had joined them or they had left their horses unguarded.

Bitter thought, that. They could stake their horses untended within a dozen feet of me right now and I wouldn't be able to reach one or to climb onto him if I reached one's feet. I was that weak. It was a major effort just to raise my head.

There wasn't anything wrong with my hearing, though.

One they called George, which of course would be Ryal. One was Ed. The third was named Mickey. I remembered then that that was what Ryal had called the man I'd seen him with yesterday.

"I tell you he *can't* have gone anywhere, George. I hit him good. You saw the blood yourself. I'm still betting he's underneath all that rock somewhere. Brought it down on himself, I'll bet."

"You just said yourself that was his blood over there. That sure isn't covered with dirt."

"So he bounced off'n those rocks maybe and got covered by what fell after. Hell, it's possible."

"Do you want to dig through all that stuff to make sure?"

"I don't think we have to. I think he's under there."

"What about you, Ed?"

"Don't ask me." This man's voice was much deeper than the others. "I wasn't up here yesterday." He paused a moment and added, "I would say it's possible Mickey's right, though. Look over there. We don't know how high those rocks sat before all that stuff came down, but he could've rode it down like a snowslide and gotten bounced off them and covered over. For that matter, he could've been flipped clean over on the other side. Anybody look over there?"

"I did." I thought the voice was Ryal's. "There's another drop."

"All right," Ed said, "how about down there?"

Another pause and some scraping in the gravel. "It's possible," Ryal said. "Not likely but . . . possible." Pause. Thoughtfully he said, "It would take a couple hours to get down there."

"I think we should look," Ed said.

"I don't know." Ryal's voice again. "Hell, though, if he is down there, he's dead for sure. No need for all of us to climb all that way down. If he's up here, he might still be alive. Ed, you go down and look in that bottom. Mickey and I will search up here again."

"We've already looked up here till I know every pebble by name and family connections," Mickey protested.

"Fine," Ryal said. "You go down that slope while Ed and I look up here."

I heard a crunching of gravel and when the voices came again they were fainter but still understandable.

"I don't like the looks of that climb," Mickey said.

Good boy, I told him in my mind. I wanted Mickey to stay up here if Ryal insisted on doing more searching nearby.

The thing was, Mickey already said plain enough that he didn't believe they would find anything, anyway. If he was doing the looking near to where I actually was, he was likely to be lazy about it.

Ed, on the other hand, wasn't familiar with the ground they would be searching. He would be looking it over with a fresh eye and was much more likely than Mickey to find something that the others had already passed over as being unimportant.

Having thought of that myself, I began to hope that Ryal would not. Happily enough he didn't.

"Okay, okay," he said wearily. "Ed, you go on down there and look it over. If you find him, give us three shots and we'll come join you."

Ed's voice said, "That's a pretty good climb. If I don't find anything an' you don't signal for me, I'll head back to camp from there. Join you later."

"If you think it would be easier."

"Lots. Look over there. See? That looks like a game trail. Hell, I can walk up that an' never need a handhold. If I'm figuring it right, that bench leads around to camp."

"Good enough then. We'll see you later, Ed."

I heard some grunting and scraping and then silence for a few moments.

"He won't find anything," Mickey said after a minute.

"I don't think he will either but he might."

"Nope," Mickey said with certainty. "That boy is under a couple feet of trash rock right now, George." He laughed. "Why, you could be standing square atop his head right now."

"I don't really believe that either," Ryal said.

"Where then?"

Ryal cursed. "If I knew that, we'd be on our way home now."

The sound of their footsteps moved close to me and closer still. They got close enough that I could hear one of them, Ryal I guessed, sigh. Criminy, they couldn't have been a dozen feet from me. They must have been leaning up against the same boulder I was hiding under.

I could hear the rustling of cloth and one of them spit. I heard the scratch and flare of a sulphur match, and a moment later I could smell the sharp, tantalizing smoke off a cigarette. Lord, what I would have given for a smoke myself.

I haven't any idea how long they stayed there, but it seemed a terribly long time.

I know for certain it was long enough that my interest and my fear wore off enough that I again became aware and more than aware of the pain in my side and the cold in my bones.

I was afraid to breathe lest they hear the sound of it, they were so close. Afraid to let my teeth chatter lest they should hear. I wanted to cover my mouth to muffle the likelihood of both, but I knew good and well if I moved at all they would hear the shift of the gravel I was lying on. They would have to hear it. They were so close I was at least imagining I could smell them as well as their tobacco.

Every once in a while one of them shifted his feet and I could almost feel it reaching me through the ground.

Something metallic, a rifle barrel probably, knocked against the boulder and I winced at the sound. That small tightening of my muscles drove pain through me like a burst of fire and I clenched my teeth against crying out from it.

The sweat popped out on my forehead again and felt like so many pinpoints of ice there.

One of them cleared his throat. Ryal it would have been, for immediately after he said, "We've stood around long enough. Let's look one more time, Mickey."

A sigh. "I s'pose."

Footsteps crunched away and out of my hearing.

The relief was so great I felt even weaker than I had before. But much better too.

CHAPTER 32

They kept drifting in and out of my hearing all that morning and on into the early afternoon. I was sore and I was sick and I guess I cried a little before I finally heard Ryal say they would go back to their camp and join Ed.

Their footsteps faded away for what I hoped was the last time, and I lay there for a while sobbing and letting the release of tension wash through me and loosen the knots that my muscles had become. Oh, it did feel good.

After a time, when I thought they'd been gone long enough or almost that long, I moved my arms for the first time in hours. They had been immobile for so long that it hurt even to do that, and I allowed myself the luxury of a groan.

Damn but that felt good.

It wasn't quite so cold now. In comparison with what it had been, it felt almost warm now. I knew the sun would be past the peak above me soon and it would cool off again as soon as it was, but for the moment I could lie there without shivering, even under my boulder.

If the cold was a little better, though, my thirst was worse. It was well over twenty-four hours now since I'd had anything to drink, and I was beginning to think it was going to drive my tongue out past my teeth. Every part of me was crying out for water now.

That rounded block of chalk-colored ice was still there before me. Tantalizingly near and really the only thing in my range of vision so I pretty much had to look at it if I had my eyes open at all.

If I could reach the blasted thing I could chip enough away to satisfy my thirst.

For the first time since I came to my senses and found myself already in here, I tried to move. I tried to drag myself forward with my arms.

It was like somebody reached a bale hook inside me and tried to rip me apart with it. Nothing could hurt that much, yet it did.

I cried out and snapped my teeth against the tears and the pain.

I've seen injured dogs bite at themselves and snap their teeth at the pain that held them. Now I understood why they did it. It was a mindless, animal thing to do and it helped not a bit, yet I had to do something, had to make some sort of gesture no matter how pointless.

The pain was like a solid thing, like it had a separate life of its own. And thinking of it like that I was able to fight it. A man can oppose anything real, and nothing could be more real than this.

I was ready for the pain this time. I knew what to expect and I knew no matter how bad it got I could endure it and live beyond it. That seemed a very good thing to know.

So again I tried to lever myself forward in the close, cramped space of my narrow, downsloping chamber.

It worked. Not by much, it was true. A man who thinks of movement in terms of yards or even of feet would find it too little to be worth mention. It was only inches, two or possibly three at the most, but it was motion. It was success of a sort and it was very much a matter for hope, and I was downright proud of myself.

The ice, though, that precious, watery ice was still several feet away from my outstretched fingertips, and even after so little gain beyond my original position I could feel my head bumping against rock when I lifted my chin; and the stone sides of the chamber were just a little bit closer to my shoulders than they had been.

The space definitely narrowed from where I lay to where the ice was. Probably that was why I had stopped where I did. As bad off as I had been I probably crawled forward like an animal until I could go no farther.

I still couldn't.

If it had just been a matter of the pain, I would have kept

trying. I could manage that. What I could not do was roll a cabin-sized boulder away from the mountainside.

I lay for a while panting and staring at the ice that was just out of my reach.

At the base of the sculptured mound of ice, I could see a shallow pool formed by the slow melt that would consume the whole block sometime before next winter brought a new formation to take its place here. I would have given anything to have been able to lap that water into my mouth, dirt and all.

If I had had any sort of tool that would extend my reach, I might have been able to chip some of the ice free and drag it to me. Anything would have done. My rifle would have been long enough.

It occurred to me then that I had no idea what had become of my rifle. I hadn't thought about it since I leaped out onto the gravel slide and felt that bullet strike. Probably the old gun was buried somewhere along the slide the way Mickey thought I had been. It still had four cartridges in it, but now I would much more have valued the barrel itself than the protection it might have given.

Wishing does little good, though, so I tried to put the rifle from my mind and pay attention instead to what I had instead of what I had lost.

Starting from top to bottom, I had little. My hat was gone and probably buried along with my rifle.

I was still wearing my vest, inadequate though it was against the cold. In my pockets I had some tobacco, papers, and matches. I had wanted a smoke earlier, when it would have been stupidly suicidal for me to have one. Now I safely could but my mouth was so dry the thought of smoking was not at all tempting. Besides if—no, when—I got out of here, I might well need my matches for more important things.

In my pants pockets I had my pocketknife and some loose change. Under my shirt was a canvas money belt containing what was left of my last winter's wages.

I was wearing a wide leather belt with a heavy buckle on it. I thought about that for a time. If there had been more room in which to swing the buckle I might have flailed it against the ice in the hope I could send some flying chips within reach. If, that is. There was nowhere near that much room around me. The best I could possibly have managed would have been a gentle toss onto the ice surface. More wishing, no results. If I was going to wish, I might as well wish for a water barrel and a soft bed. That would do me just as much good, or as little.

I began to think about that, though. I *could* manage a gentle toss of something onto the ice. Or into the bit of melted water beneath it. I couldn't hope to chip the block that way, but . . .

Quickly, my fingers shaking with excitement and weak but still working, I tugged at my shoulder with my nails, clawed and dug and pulled until I broke the seam open and slowly managed to rip the sleeve from my shirt.

I tore the cloth in half lengthwise and tied the two long strips together. Between them they were long enough.

On the third toss the cuff of what had been my sleeve reached the water and wicklike filled the fibers with the precious water.

Smiling for the first time in what must have been quite a while, I pulled the cloth in to me and stuffed the sopping wet end of it into my mouth.

The cuff yielded the water onto my tongue, a tablespoonful at most but it was water and it was marvelous good. I tossed the cloth forward again and watched with delight while it refilled itself. I had all the time it might take to quench my thirst.

CHAPTER 33

The second night was just as cold as the first had been but maybe longer. I wasn't passed out for part of the second one.

A couple things were better on this second night. The basic one of those was that I felt pretty sure that no matter how bad it got during the night, no matter how uncomfortable and hurting I might be, I probably would come out of it alive in the morning.

Ryal and his friends might find me then or, if they didn't, I might starve, but I figured I was going to live to see morning. That helped me considerable.

And of course I wasn't so thirsty now.

Oh, I was a long way from satisfied. There hadn't been much my bit of cloth could reach. But I sure did feel better than I had.

More important than the water itself, I think, was the lift it gave to my spirits. I had been feeling pretty low there, but getting to that little bit of water reminded me that I *was* still alive. I was bad hurt but I wasn't done, and maybe I *could* still make it if I just remembered to think things through and find a way to do the things I would have to do.

The first thing, of course, was to keep from being found by Ryal and Mickey and Ed.

To do that I knew I would have to stay where I was for at least another day. They might very well come back to look again, and even if I could find another hiding place as good as this one—which up on this mountain I supposed I could, in any of dozens of places—it was much less likely that I could do it without leaving a trail of some sort that they might find.

How I got in here I didn't remember very well but as best I could figure it, I was close enough to the fresh slide area so that everything had been disturbed, anyway, and tracking would have been even harder than usual. Away from this spot that would not be true.

And it is still a fact that a man who isn't moving leaves no tracks.

There was also my need for as much healing as possible before I tried to move.

Food and water are necessary for survival but so is blood. The longer I waited before I moved the less likely I would be to break the wound open and finish Ryal's job by quietly bleeding to death.

On the other hand, the longer I went without food and remained short on water the weaker I would become.

It made for an interesting balance, when to go, how long to stay.

I for sure didn't intend to leave where I was before morning. After that it would depend on whether the park's latest vigilance committee showed up then. I didn't want to take any chances on them finding me out in the open. Even if I had a gun, I couldn't defend myself if they spotted me.

So I had to wait. I pulled my vest as close around me as I could, not that it did any good to shift it but it made me feel a little better for having tried. I did my best to ignore the fact that my bare left arm was freezing. Not that I for a minute regretted tearing the sleeve off, but still . . .

But still it wasn't as bad as it might have been, I kept telling myself. And even if I did complain that my arm was freezing, the truth was that I didn't think it would be quite down to freezing at this time of year. Close to it but not quite there, I thought. Call it somewhere in the mid-30s. Heck, that wouldn't kill me. Give me a devil of a cold maybe, but it wouldn't kill me.

Anyway, I lay there and lay there and eventually, somehow, I dropped off to sleep.

In the morning it was the rising wind that wakened me. The sun was already up.

I was afraid they might have come while I was still sleeping and I was scared to move lest they might hear.

My left arm was cramped, probably from being clutched so

close against my body the whole night long, but as bad as the muscle cramps hurt I didn't dare move it to ease the pain.

I smiled then. It occurred to me that this morning a simple cramp was bothering me more than the hole in my side. Of course I wasn't moving at the time—I was a heckuva long time from being healed—but it was an improvement and that had to count for something.

I lay totally silent for an uncomfortably long time until I did hear footsteps approaching. Very light footsteps as of a small person or a large one who was trying to be stealthy and silent.

My body wasn't quite so cold now but inside me I froze.

If they were creeping up on this spot, they must know I was here.

To be found, to die, after so much already, it just wasn't fair. That was all. It wasn't fair. It was too much to waste now.

The careful footsteps slowed and moved closer. There seemed to be two of them again. One of them had a cold. I could hear the sniffing and snuffling of his breathing.

Would they haul me out and talk to me first, I wondered. Or would they just shove a pistol barrel into the opening and cut loose on me.

Oddly enough, I wondered what it would feel like to be shot. I had been shot recently enough already, but I'd been too busy at the time to notice it much. The pain had all come later, after the shock wore off.

This time there wouldn't be any later to wake up to. Not in this world, there wouldn't. And the simple truth was that I wasn't ready to enter that other one yet. There was still too much to do in this one. So much I wanted to do.

The sniffing was heavier. Very near to my feet. I guessed whoever it was was just going to shoot.

I muttered a very vulgar word to tell him what I thought of him and his.

The sniffing was replaced by a sudden, explosive snort.

The clatter of feet and legs and flying gravel sounded within feet of me and went galloping off in the distance.

My God, it'd been a deer or an elk wondering what the strange smell was all about.

I breathed deeply again and after a minute was able to laugh some at my own fright. Scared of a deer. Wasn't that a pretty pass to come to.

One nice thing, though, when I calmed down enough to realize it. If a deer was nosing around my hiding spot, it was for darn sure no man was. Ryal and his friends weren't anywhere around. They might well have given up and left the mountain for the warm comfort of a roof and fireside.

Probably had, in fact, because I didn't think they would be searching anywhere on the mountain without making this nearby end of the slide the center of their circle.

Of course it was possible they had started here before I woke up and were now searching farther out on the mountain. I wasn't going to crawl out to see for sure.

Still, the deer proved that they weren't close even if they were still looking, and if they came back I would hear them. I could permit myself some movement.

I broke out my handy-dandy shirt sleeve and helped myself to some breakfast. Which also proved that I'd been right about the temperature not quite being freezing during the night. There was again a bit of water there for me to enjoy.

When I hadn't heard anything of them by evening, I did some serious thinking on it and came to my conclusion.

It was time for me to get out of my cocoon before it became my grave. I took a deep breath and got at it.

CHAPTER 34

Getting out of there was . . . beyond description.

The narrow hole I'd gone into sloped downward from the entrance toward the ice, which meant it was an uphill climb to get out of it.

There wasn't near room enough for me to turn around so long as I was still in my little hidey-hole, so of course I couldn't get any purchase or help from my legs. And they should have been the most useful parts left of me.

Having to back out meant the whole load would be on my arms. And the heavy muscles of the shoulder seem to kind of tie in to the back. It sure felt like they did, anyway.

Lord almighty, nothing should be like that.

I cried; I yelled; I gnashed my teeth together. It absolutely wasn't worth it. Nothing could be. Except life. Which was what I would lose if I didn't get out.

If I gave in to the pain and let it beat me, let it keep me where I was, Ryal would have killed me for sure, the way he seemed to think he already had.

The choice was that simple.

If I stayed, I was dead for sure.

If I moved, I might still die: From loss of blood. From starvation. From the wound causing my guts to slowly rot away. From the shock of the pain maybe. There were lots of possibilities.

But *one* of those possibilities was that I might somehow live. It was just one of a whole lot of possibilities but it did exist. If I stayed where I was, it was not even remotely possible. Not at all.

So I clenched my teeth and tried again.

I gained an inch or two at a time, and each time I swore

and snarled and knew that mere life was not worth so much. And each time I allowed myself to collapse in despair only long enough to gain the strength for another try.

The sweat ran so heavily from my whole body that it trickled off my sides in a steady flow that I thought must be fresh blood, and I had to feel of it and check my fingertips for red before I was sure it was only sweat.

Only sweat. The damned stuff ran into my wound, and the salt might have driven me mad except by then such a pain was insignificant in comparison with the rest.

I gained an inch and an inch and an inch again; and at some time long after full dark, I felt my feet slip out over an edge of some sort and *down*. I had been moving up all this time. Down meant I had reached a lip of some sort. It meant I was close to being out.

The encouragement was marvelous. I rested less and pushed harder and the pain seemed to scarcely matter. It didn't go away, mind. But there had been so very much of it that it no longer seemed of great interest.

I cared. But not so much.

Life itself now seemed to be pain. A little more or a little less seemed of no great consequence.

So I pushed all the harder, and I gained two inches and two inches again.

My knees passed the lip and I felt around with my feet and found nothing. No hard rock confining them on each side. I was very nearly out.

I shoved myself three inches higher and did it again. Within minutes my waist was at the top, and once again I felt my knees touch gravel. Outside the hole. I was out within a minute more, lying free again and proud even if exhausted.

I burrowed as deeply as I could into the gravel and went to sleep, uncaring about the chill of evaporating sweat in the cold night air. I was free again, and I think I slept very well.

Dawn was especially pretty that next morning. It was the first I had seen for several days and I knew I was lucky to be seeing it at all.

I lay there for a while drinking it all in and enjoying being able to watch it happen. When the sun was fully up, I swiveled my head and looked up toward my hiding spot.

It was no wonder they hadn't seen it.

To all appearances it wasn't there. The gravel spill peaked right at the gap and ran onto the mountain wall. It looked unbroken and so did the contact of the boulder against that wall. I think—I wasn't in any shape to get up and look, but I think the hole would only be visible from up on the slide itself.

How I got up there to start with was something considering the state I'd been in. But then I suppose it was only the state I was in that made it possible at all. If I hadn't been in shock I just couldn't have done it.

Now my problem was a bit different, and I could have used some of that pain-killing shock.

The first order of business was something to eat and drink. I was still plenty thirsty. And, Lord, I was hungry. It had been more than two days since I'd eaten. I was beginning to notice that for a fact.

It was simple really. I could melt snow for water. And for food, shucks, I could run down one of those deer that hung around up here. No problem at all.

Which was one way of looking at it.

The truth was that I wasn't sure what I could do about food, but I did know I could get water. All I had to do was reach it, hopefully downhill and not too far.

I couldn't stand for a look around—I tried but *that* idea didn't last very long—so I just headed back toward the way I had come. I remembered skirting some snow while I was making that uphill run, so I pretty much had to find some in that direction.

And there was always the possibility that Ryal and Mickey and Ed might have thrown away some food scraps wherever they'd camped. I would probably run into the place if I went in that direction.

I thought for a moment about looking for my rifle. It would be buried under the slide somewhere. But it could've been anywhere along a four-hundred-foot fall, and if Ryal and them hadn't found it I probably couldn't either. I hitched myself on across the gravel.

At least I was able to move a little better now that I was out where my legs could do some of the work.

By driving with one leg at a time and kind of sliding along on my chest I could get a good six inches of travel with each kick. That was high-speed motion, by golly, and really made me feel like I was getting somewhere for a change. Why, I got all the way across the slide area and onto firmer ground in the first hour or so.

I rewarded myself with a short rest and began working my way up the slight rise ahead.

That was going to take longer.

CHAPTER 35

I reached a long, narrow patch of snow strung out in the shade on the north side of a rock formation. That was late in the afternoon.

It wasn't much. There wasn't a great deal of it left and what there was was old and grainy with ice. It crunched under my teeth and felt like it was burning my tongue, and it tasted absolutely wonderful.

I ate snow until I thought my mouth was going to freeze and my lips turn brittle and fall off, and I enjoyed every bit of it. It was the first time in what seemed like ages that I'd had enough water.

The other side of that coin was that it reminded me how hungry I was.

With my belly full of cold water, I could really feel how empty of food I was. One or the other, the melting snow or the basic emptiness, knotted my stomach with cramps that hurt almost as bad as my wound.

That passed eventually and I lay panting and feeling the pain-sweat evaporate coldly, and I knew that if I didn't eat something pretty darn soon I was in trouble.

It may seem kind of funny but I wasn't really thinking of myself as *being* in trouble. Just that I might be.

The thing I kept concentrating on was that I was alive. The people who'd put me here didn't know that I was alive. And I was still capable of at least some movement. Those were some pretty big pluses.

On the minus side was the fact that I was in really lousy shape.

Food seemed to be my biggest need as I was already terribly weak and getting worse all the time.

I needed warmth too. I hadn't been really warm in several days; and being weak and wounded too, I needed to start thinking about that pretty soon or I'd die of pneumonia before I had a chance to starve to death or croak from the bullet.

That was something I definitely could do something about, though.

Beyond where I'd found the snow, about fifty yards farther, I could see the gray, weathered carcass of what must have been a real grand-daddy of a tree at one time.

It took me an hour or the better part of one to reach it and by then it was coming dark.

The bark was long since rotted away, but the trunk wood itself was soft down to the fat heartwood. I dug my pocketknife out of my jeans and went to work on it. Before too long, working by feel most of the time as it got too dark to see, I had a respectable pile of burnable wood ready, much of it in long strips that chunked off once I got some finger holds started and pulled.

I stacked some of the smallest bits between me and the old log so the wood would act as a reflector for what heat I could produce, and I touched it off with one of my matches.

It caught and flickered and made me feel better just from seeing it. That handful of flame was about as pretty as anything could be. It was warm too, creating a little nest of warmth against my side where I'd built it.

It was tempting, awfully tempting, to build the fire into a real roaring, heat-producing blaze of a thing, but I knew better. A fire like that would feel just great for a few minutes but it would burn wood like I was throwing it down a well. There was no way I could feed something like that, so I resisted the temptation and added just a finger-sized piece at a time.

Then and only then did I do something I'd been wanting to do for days now. With the fire safely started, I pulled my tobacco out and rolled myself one, thinking while I did how darn glad I was that I'd taken up the habit. If I hadn't, I might not have been carrying matches in my pocket when this happened. I always used to carry them in my saddlebags along with nearly everything else.

I gave that little rascal a twist and a lick and used a piece

of my fire to set it alight. I sucked in a long, deep puff off that
smoke. . . .

And I darn near coughed my fool head off.

That smoke went down dry and nasty and like to ate me
up.

The coughing jostled the hole in my side and made things
not a bit better.

Whoever would have thought a couple days without smoking could do that to a fellow. Not me certainly.

I approached the next puff a lot more cautiously, but by the
end of that cigarette it was tasting good again, good enough
that at the end of that one I treated myself to another.

Darned if I didn't feel absolutely light-headed after that
one, so I said the heck with it all and went to sleep.

Some time during the night, while I was waking up every
now and again to find a live ember or two and rebuild my little fire, I got to thinking about something I had either heard
or read somewhere and that popped back into my mind now.

As soon as it was daylight I decided to try it. Though there
really wasn't much deciding to do. As soon as I remembered, I
knew I was going to have to try it.

Somewhere I had heard that a man could eat the low-grow-
ing moss or lichen or whatever it is that mats the dirt up here
in the high country. It isn't a grass but grows in a near solid
pad an inch or so thick in some places.

When it was light enough to see, I looked for some and discovered I'd been sleeping on a potential food supply the
whole night through. I pulled a handful up and peered at it.

It sure wasn't pretty. I put all the wood I had left and could
pull loose onto my fire and studied that stuff some more.

It was a kind of sickly gray green and definitely didn't look
like anything a sane person would associate with food. What
with the tangle of hair-thin roots and tough, dry stems, it
looked more like a handful of dead spiders than something
you would eat.

I took a bite.

It was dry and gritty but it softened a little as I chewed it.
It tasted something like a cow's breath smells.

I took another bite.

I ate that handful and another and another one after that until my jaw ached from chewing and my belly was full.

It never got to tasting a bit better and I don't know if I got all that much out of it, but I sure felt more content than I had in a while.

I pulled some more of the stuff and tucked it inside my shirt for safekeeping, just in case, and started crawling north again with my attention out for more snow to drink.

Aside from the fact that I felt like hell, I was feeling pretty good.

CHAPTER 36

I will say one thing about that moss or whatever it was. It doesn't give a fellow much strength, and that was what I needed.

I'd made maybe four hundred yards progress the first day and nearly doubled that the second, but I had to keep going late into the night to do it. And the only reason I kept going that long was because I needed to find more snow to drink and it was getting scarce.

What I finally did find might be the last I would have for a while and I wanted to tank up heavy through the night, which I did, filling myself with more every time I thought I could hold some. It made my belly ache but I figured it was necessary.

In the morning I did the same thing all over again before I started crawling.

At least there was one thing working right. The going was steeper now and all downhill. I should be able to make better time now.

By noon I was beginning to get excited. I could recognize the area where I was, and I knew I was getting close to where they shot my horse. All of my gear was there, including some real food with real nourishment in it. I needed that badly.

I got to the bottom of the slope I'd been going down, and when I saw flat ground ahead of me I started to cry. That was just too much to ask. I lay there and squeezed my eyes shut and wished the world would go away or the pain would quit or I would die or any damn thing. Anything.

When nothing did change and the world and all that was in it was still there, I opened my eyes again.

There were some trees nearby, and that wasn't so bad.
There might be some snow in the shade there.

There wasn't, of course. Of course I should remember that.
I was sitting in the shade right there when they shot old Scar
and came out of the trees off to the north where I couldn't see
from where I lay.

My God. It hit me finally. All my stuff was just ahead, probably sixty or seventy yards from me.

That was enough to bring some strength back. Enough
strength.

I began to crawl again.

The saddle was missing. The blasted, lousy, miserable,
damned saddle had been taken off the horse. And all my stuff
with it.

I kept going, stubbornly hopeful that it would all be on the
other side of the carcass, although why I thought that might
be I do not know except that I wanted it so badly.

I got up onto my forearms for more speed and ignored the
lancing pain that caused. I just had to see and as soon as possible.

I slithered around the rump of the horse and stared at the
sprigs of fresh, new grass, which were all that was there. No
saddle. No food sack. Nothing but grass and soil and dead
horse. Even his bridle was gone. Everything gone.

Lord, what a waste. How bad I needed that now and it was
gone forever from them trying to hide what they'd done. I
laid my head over against the horse's rump and closed my
eyes.

I kept thinking about something, though. Something I'd just
thought about or almost had. I kept thinking it had been
something important. I couldn't think what it was.

I kept after it as steadily as I'd kept on crawling, and eventually I reached it.

Freshly dead horse was what it was. Freshly dead.

Here I'd been lying half propped up against Scar for an
hour or more now, and I was just realizing that I wasn't smell-
ing any decay stink. He didn't stink and wasn't hardly

bloated, and it had been staying awfully cool up here as I could well attest.

I was propped up against maybe nine hundred pounds of dead animal, a majority of which was pretty much unspoiled and edible.

I'd been worried about food and here was more of it than I could eat in a month's time.

And if it was beginning to go bad, why, so what? I wasn't going to complain. It wasn't likely to kill me at this point.

I got my folding knife out and began to slice through the thick hide on Scar's rump.

I stayed there three days, gorging and sleeping and waking to gorge again. I would have stayed longer if there'd been a stream or pond in reach. As it was, water was a problem.

There was no snow under the little clutch of trees near the horse, but the ground was shaded there and I did some investigating. In a depression near the hillside there was a sheet of ice just under the ground. By chopping it out in pieces and melting it I was able to get something to drink.

It wasn't good water by any stretch of the imagination. It was more a thin mud than any kind of water, but I drank it anyway and it served its purpose.

The third day it ran out, though, and I had no choice but to move.

Anyway, my supply of meat was starting to stink.

Right at first I had stripped out some muscle layers and sliced them thin and laid them out to dry. Those I figured to carry along for a food supply while I traveled.

I was feeling a whole lot better than I had. The meat and the rest had given me back much of my strength. My chest and belly weren't near so tender.

Best of all, the hole in my side was puckered closed and was starting to heal. It didn't hurt quite all the time now and I had freer use of my arms before the pain came. Even when it did, it wasn't near as bad as it had been. I couldn't see the wound, of course, but I guessed it would take a pretty hard jolt at this point to tear it open and get it to bleeding again.

I took stock of myself and almost had to laugh. I must have looked a sight.

I hadn't shaved or combed my hair in the past week but that was the least of it.

My jeans were in tatters from the thigh down from shoving across gravel and hard rock. The insides of my boots were as bad, bare skin showing through what was left of boot and sock.

The remnants of my vest had become a sling I could carry the dried meat in, and my shirt was wrapped around my head to keep the sun off. It is surprising how much a man comes to depend on a hat when he is used to wearing one.

The lower parts of my jeans I cut off since they were just flapping around my calves anyway. I used the cloth to make knee pads that I hoped would keep me from being cut up so bad.

With short pants and practically nothing else on me, I probably looked like a bum on his way to the public baths.

Which I could use also. I smelled pretty ripe.

I was in a whole lot better shape than I had been, though, and with the water gone it was time to move.

I crawled away, at first light, on my hands and knees and proud of it. It was the first time I'd been off my stomach since I'd been shot.

It was a lot easier to make time that way, and I covered several miles before I called it quits.

The next morning I found a dead sapling that was just the size and shape to tempt me, so I tried something else and found that it worked.

Carefully, using the rough bark of a tree for support, I climbed up off my knees and onto my feet for the first time in what seemed like forever.

I swayed and I wobbled and I felt strange as hell, but I didn't fall down. I felt so good about it I rewarded myself with a cigarette and the use of a match for no more purpose than to light it.

When the smoke was gone, I took my staff and walked down away from there. Not very darn fast, I admit, but I was upright and walking.

Four days on my feet—it would have been way less than a day by horseback—and I reached the pond above the house where I used to keep my horses back when I had horses to keep.

One of my food caches was there, and I needed it bad. My dried meat had run out the morning before, and I'd only had one drink in the past two days. I was back on my knees by then.

Getting down to that cache was almost like a homecoming.

I built a fire and opened a can of tomatoes that I ate and then used the empty can to cook up a mess of beans and rice in the juice left from the tomatoes.

I laid up there for a full day eating and drinking and sleeping more than I was awake.

The next morning I picked up my sapling and went home.

CHAPTER 37

There wasn't much food in the house, but anything was plenty in comparison with what I'd had lately. Later I could pick up one of my caches or even move back up if necessary. Right now I figured I needed my bed and roof more than anything else.

With Ryal and the rest of his vigilantes believing me dead, I should be in no danger here unless I showed lights and even then only if I was unlucky. There weren't many people who normally passed this way.

I got a quart or so of water from the cistern—didn't want to carry anymore than that for I still was in poor shape and brewed up a pot of tea. I'd practically have given up my hope for heaven in exchange for a cup of coffee, but all the coffee I had was up on the mountain in my caches. So tea it was, and under the circumstances it tasted pretty fine. It was the first hot drink I'd had in a long while.

Really and truly satisfied for a change, I found a bottle of laudanum and took a pull from it to take away the last of the pain. I crawled onto my bed and slept through nearly until the next dawn.

More tea, more laudanum, and a bite to eat and I felt darn near ready to lick the world. The question was how to go about it.

The only advantage I had was that I was the only one who knew I was alive. Once I made an appearance anywhere I wouldn't have that any longer, so when I did show up in public somewhere it had better be a good one.

In the meantime, I had to be mighty careful. I didn't have a gun to defend myself if I was found, and I wasn't in any kind of shape to do any running. If I was found they had me, plain and simple.

Come to think of it, I didn't even know if I had a horse I could use when I did decide to go somewhere.

Old Scar was dead, and Slick and the dun had been run off. The only others I owned—or had owned—were the brown mare and Nero, the ancient drafter.

I didn't have a saddle either. It somehow never occurred to me before, but Pop's and Kyle Junior's stuff was never returned to me. All their gear kind of disappeared after that night, including their saddles and guns. I could have used that stuff now.

I thought about hobbling down to the horse pasture to see if I still had anything there to use, but I decided against it. It was a mile each way and that seemed too much for so little.

Besides, there really was nowhere I wanted to go right now. If I went to town, it would only put the vigilantes on warning. If I went up to Fairplay and told the law, it might well do the same.

I gave it some serious thought and finally decided my only chance might be to take Beth Sorensan's suggestion and go all the way up to Denver. I didn't know if anyone there would or even could do anything for me—and frankly I doubted it—but it was about all I could think of to do. It was faint hope and much desperation, but it seemed to be either that or buy another gun and try to depopulate South Park. Somehow I just couldn't see myself doing that.

A trip up to the next rail station north of Fairplay, though, was not something I wanted to take on just yet. It would be fifty miles or close to it and, even if I'd had the dun horse and my saddle, I wouldn't want to try that trip yet.

At least I didn't have to push myself about it now. So long as no one knew I was here, I could let patience work for me while I healed. When I was ready I would go.

I spent several days doing nothing but resting and eating. I walked out beyond the cistern just once. That was to check the horse trap, and I only went far enough to see that the horses were there—which they were, thank goodness—but not so far as to tire me out or increase the danger I might be seen.

The laudanum ran out after a couple days, but the pain wasn't so bad by then. After what I'd already come through without it, this seemed like nothing at all.

I minded worse when the tea was gone.

When I ran out of food, it was time to move again; and I decided if I was going to have to move anyway it might as well be for the railroad as for more food.

I got dressed, thankful all over again that I'd had some spare clothes at home, and pulled on what was left of my boots. Those I hadn't had spares of.

Before dawn I left the house and went down to the horse pasture. I wanted to be past the Ryal place before anyone was out and around over there. Once I was north of Ryal's ranch, I figured I could keep my distance from anyone else and shouldn't be recognized. Since I was supposed to be dead, no one would be looking for me. I'd thought about that sort of thing quite a bit in the last few days, but I didn't want to tempt fate with Ryal.

Anyway, I was down at the gate way before dawn. I didn't have a spare bridle but I had found an old snaffle bit in the boxes of assorted junk on the place and had used some of my idle time to piece together a mismatched collection of twine and old leather that should serve as one.

Nero and the mare were grazing along the fence a couple hundred yards from the gate, and I gave them some soothing babytalk to let them know I wasn't some sort of booger creeping up on them in the dark.

Old Nero has always been as calm as a lump of cold tallow; and with his presence to steady her, the mare let me walk up to her and drape my makeshift reins around her neck without a fuss.

I led her back to the gate with Nero plodding along behind for the company. He was a likable old thing.

And I guess I would have been better off if I'd gotten sentimental about the old boy and decided to straddle his wide, fleshy back for the long ride up to the railroad.

I positioned the mare beside the gate and spoke to her as soothingly as I knew how. She pinned her ears back but didn't seem too excited.

Very, very carefully, for I was still awfully tender, I climbed onto the gate and stepped across to fork the mare's bare back.

I hadn't ridden bareback since I was a kid, but like most youngsters that hadn't slowed me down any then and I was riding Pop's horses long before the folks could afford to buy me a second- or third-hand saddle.

The mare seemed nervous and, in truth, it had been quite a while since she had been ridden.

She began to fidget and dance a little, so I walked her in a few tight circles to remind her and hopefully settle her some. When one ear came forward again, I eased her back to the gate and leaned out to unlatch it.

Something, it might have been the keeper loop on the gate moving or maybe my heel brushed her flank in a way she didn't like, but something set her off.

She bogged her head and squealed, and I tried to get back in balance over her.

I was too late. She humped her back and began bucking. I almost made it back onto her, but a darn snaffle bit doesn't have any bite to it and she could do as she pleased. She pleased to buck, and she got ahead of me. I never quite got back over her.

I stuck with her for a couple jumps, but she had me out of shape and getting worse with each jump.

About all I could do was come off as gracefully as possible. I turned loose of what little hold I had.

Too late, I caught a dark flash out of the corner of my eye, and I knew what I was heading toward.

I was flung backward. The gate came rushing up toward me and smashed into the small of my back.

In the brief instant before the pain blocked the consciousness from my brain, I felt the gunshot wound being ripped open again and the lance of fire rush from that spot deep inside my body. I believe I screamed, but I had gone down into blackness before I could know for sure.

CHAPTER 38

Gray and red like morning mist covering my eyes and filling my throat. It was choking me, suffocating me. I coughed and the pain sharpened, came closer and became more real.

Air reached my lungs, though, and I opened my eyes. It was a feather pillow that had been suffocating me. The ticking cover and the familiar smell told me it was my own. How I got into bed baffled me. I sure couldn't remember doing it.

"Are you gonna live, boy?"

I thought I recognized the voice. I allowed my head to roll to the side so I could see. I was right.

Amos Gordon was lifting his bulk off one of my chairs. He came to me and felt of my forehead.

"I couldn't find any food in the house, Cyrus, nor any medicine. You got any tucked away somewhere?"

I let my eyes sag closed again. "No. All gone."

"You need something to kill that pain."

I couldn't argue with him. It was as bad this time as the first.

"When did it happen?"

"Horse threw me. Old mare. Before daylight."

"That's when you were shot?"

I started to shake my head. Just the beginning of the motion was enough to change my mind. It was easier to talk than to move. "No. That was . . . ten days, couple weeks ago. Long time now." I opened my eyes again. I wanted to be able to see Mr. Gordon's expression, but he was standing beside the bed. All I could see was the baggy material of his pants knees.

"Before the twentieth then?"

"How the devil would I know."

"This is the twenty-eighth."

"All right, before the twentieth. So what?" I remembered then. "That was the day Ryal was talking about too. What was so special about the twentieth?"

He ignored my question and asked, "You talked to George then?"

"Not exactly." I told him about it, overhearing the conversation, the race into the high country, the shooting.

He pulled a chair over and sat where I could see him while I talked. I couldn't read a thing from his face.

"Where was all this?" he asked finally.

I told him.

Mr. Gordon nodded. "I remember hunting elk up that way back when I was spry enough to do such. That's quite a ways from here."

I agreed with him.

"Do you have any proof it happened that way?"

"So you know whether it's safe to kill me now?" It just came out. I suppose I should have tried to be clever and sneaky and put up a bluff of some sort, but I just said what I was thinking.

His eyes narrowed at that and he opened his mouth like he was going to say something back, but he didn't. After a moment of staring at me he said, "I take it, then, you don't have proof."

"Not even my word since that's no good around here," I told him.

Again he acted like he wanted to say something but stopped himself. I closed my eyes.

"Don't go to sleep on me now, boy. What about you selling this place?"

That brought my eyes open all right. "I thought you'd given up on that pitch before now. I thought you'd voted to save money and use bullets instead. Or don't you people vote on such things?"

"Don't gravel me, boy. I'm not in the mood for it. You haven't sold the place then?"

"I haven't and I won't," I declared. "You can bury me on it but you can't buy me off."

Mr. Gordon grunted and sat back in his chair. He seemed to be doing some deep thinking. Probably, I thought, deciding whether to go with the buy-'im-out or the shoot-'im-up faction of the committee. There seemed to be both in operation around here.

Me, I decided it was too late for me to worry about such things. I'd never get to Denver now, and that had been my last hope.

Mr. Gordon shook me awake. I wasn't sure if it was right away or a while later.

"It's coming dark, Cyrus. I'm going to move you now. There's no way to feed or doctor you here." He chuckled. "This is the first time I've been glad I can't ride a horse anymore. At least I've got a rig to haul you in."

I didn't answer. At this point, no matter which faction he had been favoring to start with, the result seemed to be predictable. I didn't figure to see the morning sun either way.

Mr. Gordon disappeared and after a while I could hear some movement outside. He came back in and lifted me off the bed. It was the first time that I noticed I'd been stripped down to my drawers and bandaged.

He carried me outside without any apparent strain, although I am no child-sized burden anymore, and laid me face down on a nest of straw mattress and blankets that must have come off Pop's bed. He went inside and returned a minute later with my pillow and more blankets.

He tucked the covers in as gently as my mother could have done back when I was tiny. Considering what would be coming later, I didn't give the man a whole lot of credit for that gentleness.

The rig shifted violently when Mr. Gordon climbed into it. He planted himself in the center of the driving seat, and the wagon bed came level again.

"If you get too uncomfortable, let me know," he said.

I was pretty darn uncomfortable the way he'd fixed me up, but I told him I would.

The iron tires crunched forward and soon we bounced into the seldom-used ruts leading away from the house. The first jolts made me think that, in spite of the padding, I might have to call out.

Then we started to hit the rough parts of the road, and I didn't have to worry about it anymore. I passed out.

CHAPTER 39

When I came around again, the wagon was parked under an overhang next to a shed, and Mr. Gordon was no longer in it. I raised my head enough to see a few lanterns hung outside some buildings that I recognized.

Most of the places were dark, but there were lights burning outside Garrigan's saloon and the inn. The houses, nearer to me than the town buildings, were dark. I guessed it must be pretty late.

Dropping me off for Delaney and the vigilance committee to dispose of, I decided.

I tried to get onto my knees. I wanted to drop out of the wagon and crawl into a hiding place. It had worked once.

I couldn't do it. I couldn't begin to get onto my knees.

It was too late anyway. I could hear footsteps and some faint whispering.

Mr. Gordon picked me up. Whoever was with him seemed to be following. I couldn't see him anyway.

He carried me around behind a house—I couldn't remember whose it was no matter how hard I tried—and up a flight of stairs on the outside of the back wall.

It was even darker inside. Mr. Gordon shuffled his feet now, and I guessed he didn't know where the furniture was placed and didn't want to stumble into anything.

He laid me down on a narrow, hard bed, and I heard some more whispering and moving around.

Someone shut the door and I could hear blinds being pulled.

A match scratched and flared close enough to my eyes that the sudden light hurt. Mr. Gordon lighted a lamp and handed the match across me. Someone else lit a second lamp on that side.

I turned my head.

"Hello, Cy," Beth Sorensan said with a gentle smile.

Good Lord, if she was in on this too . . . I felt like a complete fool after all I had told her. No wonder they'd kept finding me. Beth was the one I'd been telling about what I thought and what I wanted and what I suspected.

She was into it too, and I'd played into their hands with every word I told her.

All that concern and sympathy she'd expressed. She must have been laughing up her puff sleeves at how stupid and gullible I was.

It seemed I never would learn about the people of this park.

I lay rigid and angry, with myself as much as with them, while Mr. Gordon and Beth changed the blood-soaked bandage Mr. Gordon had wrapped around me earlier. Beth poured some cold fluid into the wound, and they tied a new pad of cloth into place.

"I'll have to get some laudanum in the morning," Beth said in a low voice. "I've never needed any of that for my pupils."

"He's tough as a new boot or he'd already be dead up on that mountain," Mr. Gordon said. "He'll be all right till then. Anyway I'd like him clear-headed when I talk to him. All that opium stuff can take a person right out of his senses."

"All right then, but I think it should wait."

"No. Now will be better. You *are* awake, Cyrus. No point in ignoring us, boy. We need to talk."

"Why?" I guess I said it kind of bitterly.

Mr. Gordon chuckled. "See there, miss? He don't know who to trust. Prob'ly figures he can't trust anybody." To me he said, "There's some things you need to know, boy, starting with when this girl here came up to Fairplay to look me up an' give me a report on what was happening down here."

With both of them telling the story, one of them jumping in to correct the other or to add something the other didn't know about, what they told me was this:

Mr. Gordon wasn't a deputy anymore but he was still tied pretty close to the county law. He still regarded the south part of the park as his territory in a way, and he wasn't altogether satisfied with the way Jack Delaney was handling things here. Mr. Gordon also still had a lot of friends in the courthouse and enough pull with them to generally get his own way.

When what I was telling him didn't match what Jack Delaney told him, he got more and more curious.

Then Beth Sorensan came to see him and told him about me being grazed across the shoulders after leaving him that night. That was proof enough of who was telling the truth, so he decided to do something about it.

Of course about that time I dropped out of sight and didn't see Mr. Gordon again. He couldn't know what was going on up on the mountain, and I couldn't know what was happening down below.

Mr. Gordon checked the county clerk's records. Along with Pop's patent to the land title, he found a recorded copy of the survey showing the boundary between my place and what was now Ryal's. With that Mr. Gordon had enough, he figured, to hold a court hearing on the matter of the fence cutting and livestock trespass. Since Ryal had told Delaney, according to Delaney's official report, that he had cut his own fence, Mr. Gordon figured he could make it stick.

Gordon sent notice of the court date to me at the post offices in town and at Kester. Ryal was served with a notice too. Gordon had Jack Delaney serve the paper.

According to what Laura told Beth, George Ryal, Jr., was furious about the hearing. Not because of what it might cost— he could easily pay for a few miles of fence and a scrub bull— but because he was afraid of what his father might think about it all.

One hand had already quit Ryal and gone back south to the senior Ryal's huge ranch, leaving in disgust with young George but promising not to say anything about it to the old man if young George fixed things here. If the hearing went against him, young George was afraid his father would find out about that and about the hand's opinion of his son.

That would have been Jess Baker, I thought. I always had thought Jess was straight.

Anyway, the hearing date arrived but I didn't.

George Ryal, Jr., showed up in the courtroom with a triumphant manner and a piece of paper witnessed and sworn to by his two remaining hands.

According to the paper, I'd sold my place to George Ryal, Jr., for one dollar and other good and valuable considerations. It carried my signature, they said, along with the others.

With that in his hand, the matter of the fence cutting and bull were declared moot—I think that is the word Amos Gordon used—and was dropped by the court.

Young George also became something of a hero among the men of the park for getting me out of their hair.

Even so, Beth hadn't believed it and Mr. Gordon had been skeptical.

Mr. Gordon had gone so far as to search the county records for something with my signature on it to compare with Ryal's paper.

And Beth had gone through the few records kept in the school from the days when I attended there.

Neither of them had found anything with my signature on it. Mr. Gordon sure seemed upset with himself for either losing or misplacing the letters I had written him earlier.

Then a few days ago, Mr. Gordon got a letter from Denver in the same handwriting and again with my name at the bottom telling him I had forgotten to turn the old, pensioned-off horses out of the trap and asking would he see to it. That was the reason he had driven down and found me.

"That part was pretty cute," Mr. Gordon said. "I guess it wasn't any secret that I hadn't believed the bill of sale, but that letter convinced me where nothing Ryal might have said would have."

"It convinced me, too," Beth said. "Amos showed me the letter on his way down to your place. I think we were both surprised and disappointed in you, to think you'd been bought off after all."

"It would have worked," Mr. Gordon said. "Of course, Ryal thought you were dead and gone. And even if someone tried to look for you in Denver, it wouldn't be surprising that they couldn't find you in a place that size. They could assume anything they liked. Ryal knew they would never find you. Very safe. Very effective.

"As a matter of fact, if you hadn't been down by that gate I never would have seen you. I certainly wouldn't have entered Ryal's house to look around, which I thought your place was. You were lucky, Cy."

I managed a grin. "Yeah. Lucky."

Mr. Gordon spread his hands.

"What about the vigilance committee?" I asked.

Mr. Gordon shook his head. "The men around here don't like you, Cy. They don't trust you. And you embarrass them. They're good men, and you remind them of something they'd rather forget. It would be worth it to them to buy you off if they could. But another committee? No. There hasn't been one of those in the park in five years, boy. There's no way one could be formed without me knowing about it."

I sighed. I didn't exactly know what to believe, but what Beth and Mr. Gordon had been telling me sounded straight. I just didn't know.

"You look lousy, boy, but I guess if you haven't died yet you'll make it until morning. I'll come back then, miss. In the meantime, don't let anyone know he's here. We've still just got his word against young George's and his two riders."

"I won't peep, Amos. If I leave for work before you come, I'll put my key on a nail under the stairs for you. Come to think of it, I may just play sick tomorrow."

Mr. Gordon pulled a watch from his pocket and glanced at it. "It's almost tomorrow already. Get some rest, both of you. Tomorrow might be a big day."

Beth went with Mr. Gordon toward the door. I never saw him leave. The weariness of all that had happened closed over me, and I was asleep before he was gone.

CHAPTER 40

"Can you stand a few more hours without laudanum?" Mr. Gordon asked.

"I've made it this far," I told him.

It was well past noon, but I hadn't had near enough sleep or near enough healing. Still, he wouldn't be asking without reason.

"I've been busy since I left here this morning," he said with a hint of satisfaction in his voice. "I got young Pauly Titus out of bed and sent him fogging it up to Fairplay with a note. Judge Mercer should be here any time now. And Deputy Delaney should be bringing George Ryal, Jr., in any minute now too." He smiled. "Neither of them has any idea what for."

He produced a small tin bucket and said, "I brought some soup up to you. Careful you don't slop any onto the young lady's linen. No, dammit, I'll handle the spoon. Can't trust you on your own."

It was surprising the gentleness and the time he gave to the task of feeding me. He saw it through with no signs of impatience. When the soup was gone, he saw me settled and left, saying he'd be back when he could.

An hour or so later he and Beth both came in. Mr. Gordon was wearing an unexpressive face that I was beginning to take as his official expression, but Beth looked quite excited.

"Just wait, Cy. Wait until you see. It's beautiful."

"What is?"

"Both of you hush. You'll see in a minute, boy." Mr. Gordon picked me up and carried me out of Beth's room and down the staircase.

He had two men waiting there with a litter, Pete Garrigan

and a youngster with the muscles and the sunburn of a haying hand. They carried me to Pete's place and into the shade of the saloon. In spite of where we were going, Beth stayed right beside me.

The tables inside Pete's place had been shoved aside, and the chairs were arranged in the center of the room facing Judge C. W. Mercer who was seated at the center of things.

Jack Delaney, George Ryal, Mickey, and a man whose face I hadn't seen close before but who I was betting was named Ed were sitting on one side.

It was Ryal's face I was watching when I was carried in, and the look on him was all I could have hoped for.

His jaw dropped open, actually came gaping open, and he went pale as new snow.

I could see in his eyes first the disbelief and then the fury. I was supposed to be dead and he wanted me that way *bad*. Ryal swallowed hard.

He looked angry and unbelieving and, finally, afraid, all at the same time.

Mickey didn't have his boss's grit. The one named Mickey saw me and his eyes widened. He swayed once on his chair, caught himself, and lurched to his feet.

He tried to run past my litter to get to the door, but he was jerked from a dead run to a complete halt by one meaty Amos Gordon hand clamped on his arm.

Calmly Judge Mercer said, "There will be order in the court, gentlemen. Mr. Gordon, please seat the, uh, witness."

Mr. Gordon did. Mickey looked too limp to try it again.

"Deputy Delaney," the judge ordered, "place a table there on the prosecution side. Gentlemen, put the litter on the table so Mr. Tetlow can see the witnesses. Thank you. Now, gentlemen, this is an arraignment proceeding in the matter of the State of Colorado versus George P. Ryal, Jr., Michael J. Seamon, Edward Harrell, et al on charges of attempted murder. Shall we begin?"

It didn't take long at all.

I really expected it to be taut and exciting, but it wasn't. Under the judge's quiet rule it was dry and almost boring. He had me tell that I was shot but even that came out dry and calm from the way he put his questions.

It was over in just a few minutes.

The judge rapped his knuckles on Pete's bar and said there was sufficient evidence to warrant prosecution. He ordered that a charge of attempted murder be entered against the defendants and that they be bound over for trial.

Ryal asked about bail, and the judge said it would be two thousand dollars.

Ryal didn't bat an eye. He pulled a check out of his coat pocket, borrowed a pen, and wrote it out.

Then George P. Ryal, Jr., walked out of there and left his two hands to be carried off to jail in Fairplay.

That was Jack Delaney's job, and I kind of enjoyed watching him lead them out. I don't think he enjoyed it anymore than they did.

Mr. Gordon and Beth and the two litter carriers took me back up to Beth's room, where I gulped down some laudanum against the pain and went back to sleep.

It hadn't really been as big a day as I'd expected, somehow.

CHAPTER 41

Beth was having to sleep fully dressed on a settee, which was an embarrassment to me. I felt uncomfortable about putting her out like that, but she wouldn't even discuss taking me back home.

I wouldn't be safe there, she explained firmly the first time I brought it up, and besides that I was in no condition to care for myself.

The truth was that she was right about that. I don't know if I'd been weakened by the first time around with this wound or what, but this time it really had me down.

I was so weak I could scarcely raise my chin, and the hurting seemed more constant and much more annoying than it had even when I was coming down off that mountain.

Beth kept laudanum beside the bed where I could reach it and fed me all I could hold night and day, and everything she did made me feel that much worse about putting such a burden on her.

After four days of that, Friday it was, she came home from school later than usual. She looked awfully down at the mouth and no wonder. She was facing a whole weekend with a stranger in her room and an invalid at that.

"Look," I said, "there's no reason in the world why I can't be moved over to the inn now. They can take care of me just fine now after the good start you've given them."

She didn't even fuss at me the way she usually did. She just shook her head wearily and said, "Amos is in town. I saw him over at Delaney's store. He'll be up in a minute."

She slumped down onto the settee and sat without looking at me.

A half hour or so later Mr. Gordon came up. He didn't fool around with any greetings or false cheer.

"Bad news, boy. Ryal jumped his bond. He's as gone as last winter's wind. I wish I could tell you we'll get him back, but I don't know that we can. He has money to run with and if he isn't stupid he might well get away with it.

"I tried to wire his father when I heard. Ryal, Sr., is out of town and can't be reached for at least a week. I think he's helping the pup get settled somewhere with a new name and a new life. It doesn't look very promising."

I sighed. "Well, at least he won't be cutting my fences anymore."

"No. He won't."

"Mr. Gordon, the last time I saw you, you said something I've had a lot of time to think about since. It's been bothering me."

He grunted.

"You said nobody could form a vigilance committee around here without you knowing about it."

Amos Gordon looked uncomfortable. I didn't let him off the hook, though, and I didn't ask him further. I just waited him out.

"It's true," he said finally. He looked miserable. This certainly wasn't his official face.

"I like you, Cyrus. Always have. I never really wanted to have this talk with you. Like all the others, but for a little different reason, I guess I was hoping you'd leave the park and live your life elsewhere.

"You know, Cy, part of being a good peace officer is knowing when to concentrate on the law. And when to concentrate on justice." He shifted uncomfortably on his feet and rolled his hat in his hands. He wasn't looking at me.

"Something more than five years ago, several months before your dad and brother . . . died . . . I got a report from Barney Wills. You remember him?"

I nodded. Barney was a year younger than me, but we'd been in the same grade. He was a bright boy, and I'd always liked him.

"Barney had been out riding one afternoon. He'd borrowed

his daddy's field glasses and was trying to spot some bighorn sheep bed grounds. Something about making a record of their lambing rate."

That sounded like him, all right. He'd always been interested in such things.

"Well, this day he was up high on the west edge of the park and he saw some movement down below him. He watched with the glasses and he saw two men cut out a dozen calves from one of the Saylor herds. The boy had passed by that bunch on his way up and knew whose they were. He also knew the men taking them. He knew their horses and clothes."

Mr. Gordon looked unhappy but he looked at me. I think he was forcing himself to do it.

"Cyrus, those men were your father and brother. I'm sorry, boy, but Barney was sure." He looked away again.

"The men brought it to me, of course. I went over the story with the boy, and I checked the tracks on the ground. It all worked out the way he said. Kyle and Kyle, Jr., stole those calves, son. I am mortally certain they did. Believe me, I am.

"I had to follow the law on it though, son, and under the law what I had was not enough for a trial. I had a fifteen-year-old boy for a witness, and he saw it from too far away for any defense counsel not to get out from under it. There just wasn't a trial case there.

"The men of the park had been losing stock slow but steady for a period of several years. They'd been hurt. I had to explain to them that even though we knew who was doing it now—and we'd suspected it before, Cy—we still had to wait until I could catch them at it before I could make an arrest.

"Cyrus, I worked like hell trying to catch your pap stealing cows. Once he spotted me watching him. He pulled one of Virgil Beamon's cows out of a bog and then rode up the hill to visit with me and give me a lecture on neighborliness. He seemed to regard it as a game between the two of us.

"Well, I didn't mind that, and I figured sooner or later I'd get him and jail him and when he got out we'd still be friends.

"But the men of the park were the ones being hurt. Them

and their families. And when I wasn't doing any good, they formed their committee.

"I knew about it. I won't lie to you about that, son. I knew about it. I even talked to them. Warned them against it. They listened and made me no promises.

"They picked a time when they knew I'd be at the county seat for several days of court. Then they went and saw justice done."

His eyes met mine again. "Son, I tried to stop it beforehand. I swear to you I did that. I couldn't stop it. Once it was done, well," he sighed, "once it was done I had a choice. I didn't have any more trial evidence against them, Cy, than I'd had against your daddy. If I arrested them, it would go against justice and wouldn't even meet the law. It would tear the whole south end of the park apart and wouldn't help a thing.

"So I acted as a peace officer instead of a lawman. I cussed and stomped and ranted at them some, and I dropped it. There was never an official book on it. That was my decision and mine alone. If you want, boy, if it'll make you feel any better, I will resign from my clerk's job and quit eating at the public trough. But what I just told you, boy. It's the truth."

His voice had gotten stronger there toward the end. He was standing straight and looking me in the eye.

I turned my head away for a moment.

"Cy?" It was Beth's voice. "Amos told me about it a week ago. I talked to Barney. He told me the same thing. You didn't know, of course, but . . . I could ask Barney to tell you, too."

I shook my head. "No. Mr. Gordon hasn't ever lied to me. Not in twenty-one years. I don't guess he would now."

I looked at the fat, white-haired old peace officer. "Thanks for trying."

He nodded and left abruptly.

"Cy?"

"Yes, Beth."

"There's one more thing." She hesitated. "This seems to be your day for bad news."

"I'm getting kinda used to it." Actually I would have wel-

comed just about anything that would keep me from thinking
about what Amos Gordon had said.

"When George took off, Cy, he— Laura went with him.
I don't think she'll be back."

"Oh." Oddly, after all these years and all the wanting, that
meant nothing at all to me. Absolutely nothing.

Beth got up and fussed around the room in silence. After a
while she went down and carried two dinners up. She let me
feed myself for a change. We ate in silence.

Much later she asked, "What will you do now, Cy?"

"You know something? I don't have any idea. There's no
one left to fight, is there?"

"No."

"I don't know, Beth. I might stay. Try to build the place up.
And there's still that land available up north." I grinned. "I'll
be here until I heal some anyway."

My grin faded. "Beth? While I'm here . . . and if I should
stay, maybe . . . I mean, this is kind of awkward with me staying in your room and everything. What I mean is, would you
mind if I called on you? Socially, that is."

"I wouldn't mind, Cy. Not as long as you're here. Or after
you leave. If you need me, I'll be there. Wherever you want
me to be."

I closed my eyes and I started to cry, I guess. I was luckier
than I had any right to be, whatever my family's past, whatever my own future.

I reached out my hand and I felt Beth's meet mine.

Very lucky indeed.